A LOVE
FOR IVY

A LOVE
FOR IVY

•

Virginia Hart

AVALON BOOKS
THOMAS BOUREGY AND COMPANY, INC.
401 LAFAYETTE STREET
NEW YORK, NEW YORK 10003

PRINTED IN THE UNITED STATES OF AMERICA
ON ACID-FREE PAPER
BY HADDON CRAFTSMEN, BLOOMSBURG, PENNSYLVANIA

To Arlene, whose Good Sam nature and upbeat outlook on life make her an ideal romance heroine, and a constant inspiration.

Chapter One

"You can't quit." Ivy switched the telephone receiver to her other ear. "You're due at Toluca Woods Shopping Mall in twenty minutes."

"I'm sorry," the young man on the other end of the line whined. "I can't take it anymore."

"One more day. That's all I ask," she begged. "Until I find a replacement."

"Not even one more hour. Hey, seeing somebody in a giant duck costume brings out the monster in kids. One in particular kept coming back, kicking me in the shins and stamping on my feet. I've had it!"

"Brian, please. I'll give you a bonus. If you'll just—Brian?" Ivy hung up when she realized she was talking to a dial tone.

Now what was she going to do?

1

Did she have any choice? Nobody else was available on such short notice.

When she'd interviewed Brian, a science major at the local college, for the part-time job, he'd been enthusiastic about earning money wearing animal costumes and performing antics for children.

"It beats flipping burgers," he'd said.

He'd seemed to be reliable, and needing someone immediately, she'd neglected to check his employment references.

Seemed. That was the key word. But now there was no time for contemplation.

First, she had to call the part-time clerk, Florence Whittaker, who took over the store in emergencies. Fortunately, the woman was available, and would be there, she assured Ivy, as soon as she could gas up her car and advise her husband of her whereabouts.

"I can only stay till four o'clock, though. My son is coming over to help prepare me for an algebra exam."

With her last child married and out of the house, Florence had returned to school to get her degree, and wasn't having an easy time of it, partly because she couldn't understand why the school system required advanced math when she was majoring in office administration.

"What earthly good will square roots do me?" was her constant complaint.

"Four o'clock will be fine," Ivy said. "Just be sure to lock up when you leave."

Next, Ivy had to call the salesman from Gala Industries and reschedule their appointment. Then she had to scribble a hasty note to Florence about packages that needed to be gift wrapped for pickup at two-thirty.

After sticking the BE RIGHT BACK sign in the Party Animal shop window, she zoomed to Toluca Woods in her van. As quickly as she could, she changed into the papier-mâché Dandy Duck costume—not an easy task with only one pair of hands. Then, taking a deep breath, she hopped out, stationed herself in front of the Smoothee-Freeze Ice Cream store, and began a lively version of the twist.

"You're late," the proprietor called good-naturedly.

"It was unavoidable. I'll stay a half hour later," she promised, waving enthusiastically at the occupants of a passing car.

Even though they were all adults, they waved back.

"Good enough." The man squinted at the sky. "You've got a hot day."

"Tell me about it," Ivy said, already sweltering under her crepe paper feathers.

Usually entrenched behind the cash register, selling party hats and favors as well as gift wrap and greeting cards, or getting the lay of the land for an upcoming party, she hadn't worn the duck costume before, and didn't realize how uncomfortable it could be. She'd have to figure a way to allow more ventilation before anybody used it again. Maybe the fabric under the wings could be replaced with mesh.

Whew! At this rate she'd shed the three pounds she

wanted to lose, before the afternoon was over. But despite the heat and the stress of racing around, she enjoyed being out of the shop for a change.

She'd almost forgotten how much fun it was seeing the smiles on children's faces as they pointed her out to their parents, then watching the car turn around and pull into the lot for a visit to the ice-cream parlor. She liked holding out the grab bag too, allowing the little ones to choose a prize as they emerged with their cones or sundaes.

It was just that everything had happened so fast, she hadn't had time for breakfast. Ivy was a morning person by nature, and breakfast was her favorite meal. She hadn't remembered to pack herself a lunch either and her stomach was complaining.

There were no sandwich shops in this particular mall. Would a frozen yogurt bar on her noon break provide enough nourishment to keep her going?

For that matter, would she be able to eat it without removing the head of the outsized costume? Probably not, and oh, her throat was parched. She would have given half of today's pay for a nice cold glass of orange juice.

When the low, sleek car slid into the parking lot and took one of the allotted spaces, she was impressed first by the paint job—a deep metallic green that would have been her choice if she were ready to buy a new car.

But her interest in the spiffy automobile evaporated immediately when she saw the driver.

In his early to mid thirties, he was an inch or two over six feet tall. His shoulders were wide and symmetrical, she noted too, before he donned the gray sport coat he took from the passenger seat.

Was he handsome? Probably not in the pure sense of the word. But she'd never been particularly impressed by "handsome." Much more provocative were features like his—strong and appealingly placed. His eyes were gray-green. At least, she thought so. It was impossible to be sure from the distance across the parking lot, especially given the limited view allowed by the narrow slits in the Dandy Duck costume.

She could see that those eyes, though, were accented by peaked eyebrows and a sweep of faintly curling brown hair, with a bare hint of sideburns. Was he a possible Smoothee-Freeze customer? Why not? Dashing, virile types needed a refreshing break as well as anyone.

He'd noticed her too.

In fact, she found herself blushing under the intensity of his stare, until she remembered, and giggled. She'd been flattering herself. He could hardly be attracted to Dandy.

Taking advantage of the anonymity provided by her outfit, she did a clumsy time step, ending with a "tah-dah" sweep of one hand toward the newcomer.

He didn't even smile.

Okay. It wasn't the first time she'd discovered that a thought-provoking appearance didn't guarantee a sense of humor. Too bad.

She headed toward the sidewalk, deciding to make use of her childhood tap dancing lessons, and do a "Shuffle Off to Buffalo" to the corner.

"Excuse me," the man in the gray sport jacket called. "I want a few words with you."

Ivy looked over her shoulder, expecting to see someone behind her. No one was there. Did this man actually want to talk to a duck?

She touched the tip of one wing to her chest, pantomiming a "who me?"

"Yes. You." He came toward her at a brisk clip. Maybe he wanted to hire her or one of the other Party Animals for a special occasion.

She had a clown available, and a poodle, as well as a potbelly pig and a monkey. She even had access to a magician, several stand-up comics, and a mime. There were no pockets in this outfit, but she had business cards in the van if he wanted one.

He was scowling. But then, the sun was in his eyes. Maybe a dry throat he hoped to cure with a Smoothee-Freeze cone was responsible for the harsh tone of his voice.

"I have a break at one o'clock," she said as he approached. "I can see you then."

"Now," he insisted.

Who did he think he was? Okay, business was business, and a prospective customer was a prospective customer. Her dream was that eventually her self-styled animal characters would be recognized by people all over the city, and associated with her shop—

putting it on the map. That could only happen with plenty of exposure.

"Could you—" His scowl deepened, and he gestured toward her beak. "That costume is distracting. Could you take it off?"

"I'm afraid not," she said. "I can't give you more than a few minutes. As you can see, I'm in the middle of a job."

He leaned closer. "I didn't hear you."

"It would be better if you called the store later," she shouted.

He fastened his eyes—yes, they were gray-green— on her goggly blue glass ones. "This won't take long. Follow me."

She sighed, and tried a hitch kick for the benefit of two little girls coming out of Smoothee-Freeze with swirly chocolate-topped cups of frozen custard. "I'll be right back," she called, after handing each of the children a noisemaker they put into immediate use.

The speed of her prospective customer's stride didn't give her time to say anything more. She'd have to explain later. Smoothee-Freeze was one of her best customers, and she couldn't afford to antagonize the owner.

Taking two steps to each of the man's one, she trailed him through the deliciously cool corridor to a door he held open for her.

"Hold my calls," he told a woman whose desk he passed, followed closely by Dandy.

"Yes, sir," she said, lifting spidery eyebrows in

surprise, then exchanging amused glances with another woman who had been riffling through files in a metal cabinet.

"I'm Logan McKenna." He closed the door, took a seat behind an oversized desk, and indicated a chair. "Can you sit down?"

"I . . . I don't know."

"What did you say?" He leaned toward her.

"I'll see," she said louder. She backed unsuccessfully toward the chair, tried again, bending her knees, and swept a mug of sharpened pencils to the floor. "I'd better stand."

Attempting to pick everything up, she succeeded only in knocking the chair over.

"Never mind." He set everything right, and sat down again, now looking even more irritated than he had in the parking lot. "I'm responsible for seeing that everything runs smoothly at Toluca Woods."

His upper lip was finely shaped. His lower one was wide and generous, with a dent—dimple or faint scar, she couldn't tell—a half-inch to the right.

Ivy nodded, waiting.

"You're a girl—a female?"

She nodded.

The dimple deepened, as he considered her. "To get to the point, I'm not happy with your behavior."

Had she heard him correctly? "How do you mean?"

"Does it surprise you that I received complaints about you yesterday?"

"Yesterday? What kind of complaints?"

"I was informed that you lost your temper, made a scene, and screamed at the children in the parking lot."

Ouch. Brian had sounded upset on the phone, but she hadn't realized he'd blown up on the job. "Oh— really?"

"Really."

She considered informing him that he had the wrong duck. But even if she could make herself understood through the layers of paste and paper, nothing would be accomplished. As owner of Party Animal, she was responsible for the actions of her employees.

"Then, if that wasn't bad enough, you deliberately popped a little boy's balloon and had him crying." McKenna drummed his fingers on the desk.

"How can you be sure it was deliberate?"

"There were witnesses. The safety pin was wielded with malice, I'm told." He demonstrated with a twist of his wrist.

Ivy thought back to her conversation with Brian that morning about a child who had given him a hard time. Obviously he had retaliated. "He was behaving abominably," she said.

"Then you're admitting it was deliberate." His voice held an irritating touch of "Ah-ha!"

"From what I understand, it probably was," she admitted.

He leaned closer again, in his effort to hear, she supposed. "What do you mean, 'probably'? Don't you remember?"

"He wouldn't stop tormenting Dandy and . . ." She cleared her throat. It felt raw from the strain of shouting.

McKenna's dimple deepened again, this time with faint amusement. "So you're claiming self-defense? Against a six-year-old?"

"I am. Under the circumstances."

"Not according to what I was told." He shifted in his chair.

"No one would deliberately pop a little boy's balloon without good reason."

"My thinking exactly." His eyes were roving over her neck and shoulders now as he tried to decide where to aim his scathing looks. "That's why we're here."

"Mr. McKenna," she tried. "I realize . . ."

He held up a hand to cut off her argument. Stripes of sunlight filtered through the vertical blinds, making his tan look even more toasty than it had outside. "Dandy, is it?" he asked.

She nodded.

"If you can't handle children with a little diplomacy, Dandy," he said, with the exaggerated patience he might have used with a child, "you shouldn't be working with them."

Silently she counted to five before she spoke again. His striking appearance or not, she didn't enjoy being on the end of an undeserved lecture. "I know perfectly well how to handle children."

"That's open to debate. You must realize that this sort of thing reflects on the other businesses in the mall."

Protesting Dandy's innocence would get them nowhere, Ivy decided. Besides, she couldn't be sure what happened. She had only Brian's side of the story.

"That's true," she managed, mulling over what he'd said. "And I'm sorry."

"I should hope so. Even considering a certain righteous indignation, you must have a vicious temper." He shook his head, undoubtedly pondering her sins of the day before.

"Not usually."

"It's reserved for children, then?"

"Of course not," she sputtered. "I'm good with children."

"Not yesterday, apparently."

"If I didn't love them, I wouldn't have—"

"Please." Again he held up his hand, as if he were a policeman stopping oncoming traffic.

It was stifling hot under the costume and now she was beginning to itch. The way the wings were attached, though, she wasn't able to scratch effectively.

She bit back the argument that came to the tip of her tongue. What did it matter what he thought? The important thing was to get on his good side so she didn't lose this location. It was a busy mall, and centrally located.

"It won't happen again," she said instead. Unable

to take the itching anymore, she backed up to a file
cabinet and tried to move her shoulders back and forth
against a corner of the metal. It didn't help.

With an air of impatience, McKenna waited until
she'd finished. "I'm strongly tempted to tell you not
to come back."

Now he had her full attention. Could he do that?

Logan McKenna. McKenna, she thought, zeroing in
on the nameplate in front of him.

Of McKenna & Howard? The developers who owned
this and two other malls whose stringent policies had
already cost her several jobs?

At the East Side Minimall someone had complained
about children who, drawn by the Party Animal monkey, had clogged traffic and made parking difficult for
customers. No amount of argument had helped.

At the Fashion Center Complex, too much noise had
been the reason the florist who regularly used her services gave for not hiring her Toodles the Poodle to rep-
resent them anymore.

"I don't care myself," the proprietor had told her.
"But McKenna & Howard have the last say. If I go
against them, I might lose my lease."

"Who is McKenna & Howard?"

"The developing company who leases the shops.
They don't want any waves—you know. It's too bad.
Toodles was good for business."

She'd tried calling the company office to plead her
case, but had only been put off by a secretary. Now
McKenna & Howard was striking again.

"At best, your presence is a distraction," McKenna was saying.

"Distraction isn't the word I would use."

"What word *would* you use?"

"Attraction." She cleared her throat again, and tried to aim her voice more effectively through the hole that was Dandy's mouth. "I attract people to Smoothee-Freeze. But when they buy ice cream, they notice the other stores too. It's good advertising for everyone."

His scowl said that he wasn't convinced. "Some of the merchants may not care for that kind of attention."

"How could they not like free advertising?" She extended her arms—wings—to the sides.

"You don't think some may consider it undignified?"

"I can't imagine how anyone could be so—so totally lacking in a sense of humor." *Present company excepted,* she didn't add.

"The remarks you were quoted as making could hardly be considered funny."

She winced. "Maybe not. But how would you react to being kicked?"

"I wouldn't react well. But then, I don't make my living by dressing in a duck costume."

A tap at the door caught his attention, and one of the women from the outer office looked in. "Sorry to bother you, Mr. McKenna," she said, obviously trying not to laugh at the ludicrous conference. "I need your initials on this."

Logan nodded, as if nothing unusual was happening, and scribbled something on the paper she laid on the desk before him.

"And this." She removed one sheet and pointed, pressing her lips together and not looking at Ivy. "Thank you."

"If we were discussing pizza parlors or hamburger stands, it might be a different story," he continued, when they were alone again. "But most of the shops at Toluca Woods are adult-oriented. The optometrist, for example, deals with many senior citizens, who might not care for children underfoot. The beauty salon. The jewelry store."

"Most older people enjoy children."

"I'm much too busy to bat this thing around with you." He moved his chair back and stood up, indicating that she was about to be dismissed. "For now, I'll hold off on a final decision. In the meantime, see that nothing like this happens again."

His maddening "Or else" hung heavily in the air between them.

"May I go now?" Ivy asked sweetly.

"By all means." His gaze was sharp enough to cut an extra hole in Dandy's feathers. "Just watch your temper."

"Watch your temper," she muttered to herself as she took her place outside again. On the one hand, he was right. Brian had been out of line, and she'd have to stress the need for behavior more becoming to a duck when interviewing new employees after this.

On the other hand, Logan McKenna could have been less—oh, less arrogant about what had happened.

After the refrigeration in his office, the outside air hit Ivy in the face like the blast of a furnace. The sun-baked asphalt of the parking lot felt like a barbecue grill on the soles of her feet, even through her shoes. Maybe if she moved to the sidewalk it would be better. There was a small square of shade from the Toluca Woods sign.

"Look, Mommy," a small voice called from somewhere, though Ivy seemed to have lost her sense of direction. "A duck! A duck! I want my picture taken with him."

She gripped one of the metal supports of the sign to steady herself.

"Honey, I don't have a camera," a woman said.

"Let's go home and get one."

"We can't."

"Please, Mommy."

Ivy tried to walk, but her feet wouldn't move. Her eyes burned, and she felt lightheaded. She clenched her fists, trying to control the wave of dizziness that assailed her. It didn't work. She had to have a glass of water.

Maybe if she retreated to the McKenna & Howard office for a few minutes . . .

"What's wrong with Mr. Duck, Mommy?" she heard the child say, the small voice echoing in a swirl of colors.

Then she heard nothing at all.

Chapter Two

Ivy blinked, and blinked again. Something wet covered her forehead and part of her left eye. Ice water dribbled along the sides of her face and down her neck. Even her shoulders felt soggy. Somebody was waving a newspaper in front of her nose, and overhead was an unfamiliar ceiling. Pebbly white and flecked with silver, it was like the surface of an unknown planet in an early sci-fi movie.

"She's awake," a woman whispered.

"Shouldn't we call 911?" Another hushed voice.

"No, don't." Ivy tried to sit up, but a wave of nausea forced her back again.

"You fainted." The woman's face floated before Ivy's eyes. Her lips, painted a blackish purple, stretched into a reassuring smile.

16

"It's the heat." Another face, younger but equally curious, floated in beside the other. "There've already been ten heat-related deaths in St. Louis, I heard on the radio. They said—"

"Shhh!"

Ivy fumbled with the washcloth that still dripped water, but someone caught her hand.

"Leave it, honey," the woman with the purple lips said. "You might have heatstroke. Shouldn't we call someone?"

"Could I have a glass of water?" Ivy managed.

"Water, yes. Would somebody . . . no, I don't think ice water in her condition. Get some from the tap."

"My condition is fine. I only—"

"Shh." The woman pressed a purple-polished fingertip to her lips.

"That's enough. Stand back and let her breathe." The man's voice was deep and authoritative. "Time to get back to work. And hold my calls, please."

The hand that held the paper cup was square and masculine. The watch on the wrist was old-fashioned with a plain leather band.

The face that went with the hand belonged to— *gulp*—McKenna. Logan McKenna. The memory of what must have happened in the parking lot struck, and Ivy choked explosively, spewing water at him.

"I . . . I'm sorry," she tried, but the attempt only made her choke again.

"Don't swallow too much all at once. Easy does

it." He whisked away the cup before she'd even begun
to quench her thirst, and wiped the water sprinkles
from his face with the back of his hand.

Now he was giving directions on how she should
drink?

"I've fainted before," she said. "I'll be fine in a
minute."

"You've fainted before?" One shaggy eyebrow
lowered. The other peaked, giving his expression a
touch of the quizzical.

"Everybody's fainted at one time or another."

"I haven't," he said.

"Everybody but you," she muttered. Why did this
have to happen here of all places?

"You're cold." He shrugged out of his jacket and
attempted to spread it over her.

"Don't. I'm not cold." Yes, she was, she realized
the moment she'd said it. Her arms were allover goose
bumps.

Waiting until she'd settled down, he came at her
with the jacket again, and this time she didn't struggle.
"Lie back, until you get your strength."

She drew a long breath, but her throat was so dry,
it emerged as a quivering sigh. "I'd like my water."

"Not yet. Close your eyes and concentrate on
breathing slowly—in and out."

"You only have to be careful how much you drink
when you've been severely water-deprived," she rea-
soned. "When you're lost in the desert, or . . ."

"Or if you've been standing in 100-degree-plus

weather dressed in a ridiculous costume that doesn't allow your skin to breathe.'' He caught her wrist and pressed two fingers to the general location of her pulse. ''A bit rapid, but it's steady.''

Now he was a paramedic. ''May I have my water?'' she tried again.

''Of course.'' Deciding to humor her, he sank onto the couch, eased one hand under her shoulders, and brought the cup to her lips with the other.

With his proximity came the scent of spice, vanilla, and other delicious but indefinable things that must have made up his shaving lotion. What kind was it? she wondered dizzily, trying to drink from the cup that still wasn't being held close enough.

Moaning in frustration, she caught the hand, and forced the cup to her mouth.

All at once she thought of something and jerked her arm back, striking Logan in the process and sloshing what was left of the water on his slacks, as well as his jacket sleeve.

''Oh no!'' she wailed as he leapt to his feet.

''Darn it, I have a meeting this afternoon.'' Muttering under his breath, he brushed at the darkening wetness. ''What's wrong now?''

''I broke my tail.''

He rolled his eyes toward the ceiling. ''You didn't break anything when you fell. Witnesses said you crumpled to the sidewalk in slow motion.''

''I'm talking about Dandy's tail. I'm lying on it. And the wires aren't strong.'' It was a new costume.

She'd worked on it for weeks, from a pattern of her own design.

"Shh. Forget it for now." He smoothed the jacket around her again, turning it so the wet part wasn't against her chin.

"Stop telling me to shhh. I appreciate your help, but I'd better be on my way."

She felt stronger. Now that she'd been allowed enough liquid sustenance, there was only a faint throbbing in her temples to remind her of her temporary incapacity.

The women had left the office on command. Now there was only Mr. McKenna, studying her with eyes like green magnets. "What's your name?"

"Ivy." How could she be thinking of his eyelashes at a time like this? she marveled. But in her defense, how could she miss them? They were a thick dark brush, straight to the tip, and enviably long.

"Ivy . . . what?" He patted his pocket. Looking for a pen? It wasn't there. In the struggle with the water cup, it had fallen. Now it was lying on the floor under his desk. She decided not to mention it.

"Just Ivy." If she told him her whole name, he'd use the information to try to notify her parents—anything to get her off his hands and out of his office.

The next thing she knew, her father would be on his way here to expound on "female hard-headedness." With him, the two words always went together, seldom one without the other. Her mother, with tear-brimmed eyes, would be nodding and agreeing with her helpmate, as if he knew the secrets of the universe.

Dandy's head. Where was it? There, across the room, under the window.

"You didn't damage the fastenings taking my head off, did you?" she asked. "They're tricky."

"Would it matter? You're not going to put that thing on again, are you?" Logan didn't wait for an answer. "You said you've fainted before."

"It runs in the family."

"Wearing a duck costume?"

"Fainting."

She'd fainted in first aid class in the ninth grade when the teacher was describing in excruciating detail how to apply a tourniquet. That episode had gained her notoriety in school as "the one least likely to become a doctor." She'd fainted again at a horror movie when a bloody hand, severed in a car accident, scampered around strangling people. Her last blackout had been in college, when she broke her thumb in a volleyball game.

"You're saying there's a 'fainting gene'?"

"Why not? You can inherit the ability to play the piano or tennis."

"You inherited the ability to faint?"

He was making fun. But she was serious. "My mother always faints at the sight of blood." It was a habit that had endeared her to Ivy's father, because he considered it a frailty of properly feminine women, who needed male protection. "Once when I cut my finger, she—"

"Speaking of your mother, where is she?" Logan interrupted, about as subtle as a snow plow.

"She's—" Ivy broke off just in time. "Why do you want to know?"

His eyes were calculating, and his voice quiet—too quiet. This was interrogation with a purpose, not simply interest. If she identified the home base of her parents as Sedalia, it might take him a step closer to discovering her identity and bringing them here.

"Don't you think you should go home and make up with her, and with your father?" he asked.

"I don't have a quarrel with my parents." She did. But not the way he meant.

It was a running quarrel that had continued over the years, ever since she'd made her first decision that overrode that of her father. She'd been four years old and had chosen chocolate pie in a restaurant, when he thought she should have peach. But that was none of Logan McKenna's business.

"How old are you?" he asked.

Another personal question. "How old are *you*?" she shot back.

"How *old* are you?" he asked again, as if repetition would reinforce his intimidation. He drummed his fingers on an admirably muscled thigh.

"I'm over twenty-one. Five years, in fact."

His expression was skeptical. "You don't look it."

"I probably don't even look human." She took the washcloth off her forehead and draped it over the side of the wastebasket. "How could anyone possibly guess my age? Besides, I've been on my own for a long time.''

''Maybe that's your problem.''

''I don't have a problem. Look.'' She tried to sound logical. The wooziness that had felled her was fading, and her headache had subsided. ''I fainted because it was hot. Didn't someone say a minute ago that people have died in this heat wave?''

''You could have been one of them.''

''Not likely. Did you carry me in here?''

''With the help of a couple of others.''

She swallowed hard. ''It took three of you to lift me?''

''You were a bulky package.''

''Thank you,'' she said, visualizing a group of grown men puffing and blowing as they struggled to get her through the door.

''And I couldn't figure out how to get the duck suit off.''

Maybe he was persisting in this line of questioning because her thank-you hadn't been effusive enough. Sir Galahad wanted his chivalry rewarded.

''I appreciate your rescue,'' she said, with all the feeling she could muster. ''But I don't believe I was in any danger. I hadn't eaten for a long time and . . .''

His frown deepened still more. ''How long has it been since you had a proper meal?''

''I—I don't remember.''

There'd been an amateur show at the Alamo Club the night before, and she'd been contracted to supply the talent. To make sure all contestants checked in as promised, she'd dropped by. One of her singers, the tenor who won first prize, had car trouble and she'd had to drive him across the bridge to Illinois.

By the time she got home she was too tired to bother about fixing dinner. She'd downed a glass of milk, eaten a stale cookie, and decided to make up her nourishment with a big breakfast. But then Brian had canceled his appearance at Toluca Woods and she'd had to forget it.

She didn't feel like explaining all that to her inquisitor and she was sure he didn't want to hear it. He was a younger edition of her father, she guessed, and cared only about the bottom line. Forget the whys and the hows of getting there.

Logan studied her as he wadded the paper cup and tossed it at the wastebasket. It missed.

"Excuse me a minute," he said. With that, he sprang up, crossed to the door, and disappeared.

Briefly, Ivy considered retrieving Dandy's head and making a getaway. Her hero was back too soon.

"I've sent out for something to eat."

Without asking?

"I'd rather not eat now." Surely he'd understand that she felt more grimy than hungry. She needed a long soak in a perfumed tub before she even thought of putting anything in her stomach.

"Don't be stubborn. I've ordered for both of us." He clapped a hand to the back of his neck. "I'm not sure you should be eating hamburgers and fries, but that's all I could get quickly. At least it'll sustain you.''

And he would question her while she wolfed everything down.

High heels click-clacked outside the door, and the woman with the purple lips looked in apologetically. ''I know you asked me to hold your calls, Logan, but there's one you have to take. Halver on line two.''

''Right.'' He laid a reassuring hand on Ivy's arm, and patted. ''The food should be here soon.''

''I'll try to hold on,'' she whispered with a touch of Camille, deciding not to argue that she wasn't in the final stages of starvation. Couldn't he see by looking at her that missing a meal or two wouldn't kill her? She considered her costume. No, she supposed he couldn't. No one would have been able to guess her weight within forty pounds.

As she watched, she found herself fascinated by the man's body language. He paced as he talked, and used his hands freely for emphasis—slicing and chopping, making fists and waving.

The conversation had something to do with renovations that were supposed to have been finished at the end of the week in a store on the South Side. The new tenant was talking breach of contract.

''Get over and set a fire under the contractor,'' he ordered. ''No, wait. What's the number? I'll call him.''

As she waited, Ivy studied the painting on the wall

beside his desk. It was all reds, yellows, and blues splashed on the canvas every which way and signifying nothing. This was his idea of art?

By the time he'd finished his third call, the sandwiches were here, and they smelled wonderful. Scooping magazines off a side table, he pulled it over to the couch, along with a chair he set opposite her. Methodically, he divided everything, handing her napkins and packets of catsup.

"Can you sit up?" he asked, trying to elevate her head with cushions he had collected from the other, smaller couch across the room.

"Yes," she answered, waving him back. Next he'd be trying to feed her.

"You didn't tell me your last name," he said, trying for casual, after taking a healthy bite of his sandwich.

She picked up her own hamburger and rewrapped the lower section, so it wouldn't drip on her feathers. "No, I didn't."

"What is it?"

"It's immaterial."

"An unusual name."

"Funny," she hooted, taking a bite.

"Are you really over twenty-one?" he asked, undoubtedly believing that in her desperation to fill her gnawing stomach, she'd let her guard down and confess.

She waited until she took another bite of hamburger, and dabbed her mouth with a paper napkin. "I could show you my driver's license, but it's in the van."

"You live in this van?" His voice dropped, as if that bit of information explained her predicament.

"Live in it, no," she sputtered. "Just because a person . . ."

"I'm not criticizing you, Ivy. I'm only asking. Eat." He jabbed a finger at her hamburger. "Where *do* you live?"

"Where do *you* live?" she shot back, wishing she had the money with her to pay for the hamburger, if he thought the price of the meal entitled him to reams of personal information.

"I'm not fainting on street corners for lack of food."

It was time—past time—to explain the events of the day to him. "I appreciate your help, Mr. McKenna, but you've jumped to an erroneous conclusion. It's laughable, actually, but—"

"Eat."

"How do you expect me to eat and answer questions at the same time?"

"Good point. Take your time." He'd finished his own fries and was now stealing hers, drowning them with catsup until they were unrecognizable.

"I realize the economy is slow," he was saying. "And jobs aren't easy to come by, especially if you have no skills. Typing should be a requisite course for male *and* female students."

"Who says I have no skills?"

"Oh, I forgot." He snapped his fingers. "You've mastered the art of twisting balloons into animal shapes."

"It isn't as easy as you think."

"And you do a mean time step."

"Maybe I have a few skills you don't know about."

"I'm sure you do." The speckles of gray in his eyes swirled as he pondered the scenario he'd invented for her problem. "Would I be right in assuming that your folks aren't in St. Louis?"

If he wanted to play Twenty Questions that was his prerogative. "Yes, you would be right."

"Surely you can see that the sensible thing would be for you to go home and finish school."

"Mr. McKenna, I've already finished school, and then some. In fact, I have a—"

"But it's none of my business," he interrupted, holding up one squarish hand.

At that moment the woman with the purple lips swept in apologetically, and handed him some papers. He frowned at them, laid them on the desk, and scribbled on three places his secretary indicated with the point of a pen.

"If you're determined to stay," he went on, when the woman had left them alone again, "maybe you should consider a career change."

"I like my career fine. It's more enjoyable than anything I've done before, and I've had a lot of jobs."

He shook his head. "Maybe you should look beyond 'enjoyable.' "

Exactly what her father had said when she sprang the news about wanting to open a party shop. "Why should I?"

He wasn't listening. "Maybe I can help."

"Help how?" She narrowed one eye.

"I might be able to get you a job. Filing. It would be minimum wage, of course."

"Of course. What else could someone like me expect?" she retorted, deciding to abandon her explanations.

"But undemanding. You'd have time to take classes at night and improve your situation."

"I don't want to take classes at night, and I'm not a file clerk."

"You know your ABCs, I assume."

She pressed her lips together, not able to ignore the insult. "I think so. My first grade teacher taught me a song that helped me remember."

He nodded. "Good. I know of a possible opening not far from here."

"I'm not interested."

"Naturally, as I'd be recommending you, I'd want you to conform to office rules and show up on time." He gathered his sandwich wrappings and dropped them in the bag. His smile didn't reach his eyes. "You wouldn't want to make me look bad, would you?"

"Never."

"Finish eating. I have to consult with someone."

"Not about me, I hope."

"I'll be right back."

And I'll be long gone, she silently told his retreating form.

Moving carefully off the couch, she tried her legs

to make sure they worked. Then she crept over to get Dandy's head. So far, so good.

She wouldn't be able to depart the way she had arrived. One of the office workers would spot her and raise a hue and cry. Maybe Logan was even at the end of the hall, ready to give chase.

But if she remembered correctly, there was the emergency exit around the corner to her left. She'd seen the reflection of the light in the glass on her first visit.

If she could only slip past the glass cubicles, the rest would be a piece of cake if she moved fast. Could she? Considering the heat outside? Or would she only faint again and bring herself twice the trouble?

Carefully she eased the door open. The woman with the purple lips was stational at a computer. The other was at the file cabinets. Bending low, Ivy sped down the hall.

She'd made it. Taking a deep breath, she hit the bar that released the lock. As the door gave under the weight of her shoulder, an alarm shrieked. In seconds people would be swarming all over her.

Ignoring the blast of heat that met her outside, she raced to the corner and down the alley. Thank goodness she'd worked out her bearings in her mind before she left. And there was her van.

Not bothering to change out of her costume, she tossed Dandy's head in the passenger seat and turned the key in the ignition.

She was free.

Chapter Three

" "What happened to you?" Florence clapped a hand to her mouth in horror as Ivy swept in.

"There's a heat wave," Ivy threw back at her. "Haven't you heard? You make me feel like the Ghost of Christmas Past."

"If the Ghost of Christmas Past had looked like you, Old Man Scrooge could never have stood the shock. What happened?"

"It's a long story." Now Ivy was getting irritated. She couldn't look *that* bad.

"Run along home before you scare the customers away."

"What customers?"

The shop was empty, and probably had been for most of the day. Even with the circus atmosphere she'd tried so hard to create, partnered with fair prices

31

and a well-planned inventory, it was difficult to compete with one-stop shopping offered by minimalls that were springing up everywhere like mushrooms— thanks to people like Logan McKenna.

Florence shrugged. "It's been slow."

"What else is new?" Ivy pushed the bathroom door open, clicked on the light, and gasped at her own reflection.

She'd been wrong. She *did* look that bad. Her face was blotched with red. The mascara she'd unwisely applied that morning made circles under her eyes and streaked down her cheeks like war paint. Her honey-brown hair, naturally fine and straight unless coaxed, was plastered to her head.

She leaned on the sink with both hands and laughed in spite of her embarrassment at the remembered encounter with Logan. Inside herself she'd been halfway wondering if he was as attracted to her as she'd been to him.

"What's so funny?" Florence wanted to know.

"You're right. I'd better go home." Briefly she gave an account of her day, from her first meeting with the Mall Master and his trying to arrange a new job for her, to her ensuing escape.

"The way things are going here, maybe you should consider taking him up on his offer," Florence said wryly. "Your messages are on the spindle. There's a possible booking for Jingles the Clown at a birthday party next week."

"That's something."

"This McKenna must be a pretty nice guy, offering the likes of you a job." Florence picked up a bolt of wrapping paper someone had left on the counter, and began to reroll it properly. "Good-looking, was he?"

Ivy spoke carefully, wanting to be honest. "If he didn't open his mouth, he might be extremely attractive."

"His voice is nasal—squeaky?" Florence went back to the wrapping paper section to put the displaced roll in its slot.

"The problem wasn't his voice."

"Maybe you're too particular." Florence snorted. "Go home. I think I can study, and still handle this onslaught of customers."

"I think you can too."

"If you've got a minute, would you show me where I went wrong on this problem?"

Ivy studied the notebook the woman handed her, and nodded. "You didn't find the prime factors of thirty-six."

"I thought I did."

"Nine isn't a prime factor."

"Oops. You're right." Florence scratched a place between her eyebrows. "Any wonder I'm taking summer classes to catch up?"

"Where's Spiffy?"

"Sleeping in the shower stall. The coolest spot in the house."

The cat, a stray who'd already purred his way into Ivy's heart and home and who now could afford to let up on his displays of affection, opened one yellow eye when she yanked back the shower curtain.

"You ought to make the landlord fix the air-conditioning," Florence called. "It isn't much better in here than it is outside."

"And have him raise the rent? I'm barely squeaking by as it is." Ivy scooped up the gray bundle of fur and deposited him in his pet carrier. "Okay, fella. Time to go home."

The answering machine was blinking when she let herself in, and the luminous dial announced that she'd had four calls. Not yet prepared to deal with her messages, she released a disgruntled Spiffy from his carrier, opened a can of tuna cat food, and spooned it in his dish. Then she stepped out of her shoes and headed for the shower. Washing away the day took priority over all else, and she was too bone weary to even run the fragrant tub she'd visualized.

After rubbing herself dry, she put on a shorty nightgown, though it was only five o'clock. It was the most comfortable thing she owned, and she needed comfort badly about now. Then she blow-dried her hair, flipping up the silky ends where they brushed her shoulders.

Not until she'd finished a cup of scalding black coffee, and poured another, did she press the button on the answering machine and sit back on her scruffy canvas couch to listen.

"I hate to talk on these things," her mother complained as usual. "I wanted to remind you that you promised to come home for your father's birthday."

Ivy groaned, and took another sip of coffee. Had she promised? At such celebrations, her relatives, divided by long-ago sins on one side or the other, spent most of the time making accusations. It invariably ended with someone slamming out of the house in a rage, and others not speaking to each other for months—sometimes years.

The machine beeped, cutting Sylvia Canfield off. But in seconds she was back again. "I bought you a gift to give your father. A battery-run vacuum cleaner for the camper."

"I'll buy my own present, Mother," Ivy said under her breath, as the woman went on and on about how practical the cleaner would be on trips.

A male voice rumbled in the background, assuring her that her father already knew what his birthday present would be. Not big on surprises, the Canfields. Then her mother was back again.

"Dad said to remember to fill your gas tank before you start out. And check the air in your tires. We love you."

The next message was from the video store where Ivy had ordered a copy of *Breakfast at Tiffany's*. It had arrived, and they'd hold it for her until the next night.

The last call was from Ron, good friend and occasional date, wanting her to go to his company dinner on Saturday night.

"I'm being presented with a plaque for multiple sales and you'll get to hear me make a speech." He laughed. "Let me know as soon as you can."

She would. That is, she'd tell him that she couldn't go with him. He wasn't Quasimoto. In fact, his Lord Byron good looks turned a respectable number of female heads. He was funny and outrageous, and his good-night kisses were comforting.

But she'd come to the point in her life where comforting wasn't enough. Ivy wanted more—much more—or forget it.

While the eyes were the windows of the soul, as they said, she'd always been a mouth person. A mouth was more expressive, in her opinion, because true feelings could more readily be disguised in the eyes.

Even while the eyes twinkled with apparent good spirits, lips might be pulled tight in resentment, or pressed together in thoughtfulness. They could twitch at an inner humor, or lift at one corner to show disdain otherwise hidden.

Logan McKenna's mouth was full and finely carved. It had a show-me expression that was at the same time teasing. Given another scenario, she had no doubt its kisses were magic.

Okay, so she admired his mouth. Admitting that much would be the end of it. She had more important things to consider.

And Ron could wait. If he didn't hear from her, he'd pull out volume four of his little black book and dial another number, without shedding a tear. First, she had to apologize to the manager of Smoothee-Freeze for Dandy's imposition.

"Everybody's talking about it," he chortled when she'd finished her story. "If you want to know the truth, we got more customers today when people came to ogle at what was going on, than we would have if you'd put on your regular show."

"Thanks a heap," she muttered.

"I don't suppose I could convince you to pull a fainting spell every day."

"You're darn right, you couldn't."

"Don't come in tomorrow," he went on. "Give the thermometer a chance to drop a few degrees. Customers aren't out in this weather anyhow."

How understanding he was, she thought as she put the phone down—the exact opposite of Mr. High-and-Mighty, Logan McKenna. Logan was clearly the superficial type who cared about nobody but himself.

So why did she keep thinking about him?

Orders that needed mailing and a long line at the post office made her over an hour late opening the shop the next morning. One advantage of being her own boss was that no one would berate her for it. But it was a dubious advantage—no irate customers stood at the door either, hammering to get in.

After releasing Spiffy for his morning prowl and putting away the kitchen supplies she'd bought, she flicked the feather duster over the dolls in the window. Noticing that Raggedy Andy had fallen over, she leaned in and set him right. Then she stationed herself at the counter. Hoping not to look too desperate to any customers who might wander in, she pored over the previous day's receipts.

The phone rang, but it was a wrong number. A second call came almost at once, from one of her amateur performers, disgruntled because he hadn't won first prize at the contest.

"That pretty-boy singer has a range of about three notes," he complained. "I got more showmanship in my little finger than he has in his whole body."

"Your impersonations are fantastic," Ivy agreed. "But you're still doing James Cagney."

"So what's wrong with that?"

"Can't you work up something more up-to-date?"

"Humph. Nobody can imitate this new breed of actors. How can you do Kevin Costner or Tom Cruise? They got nothing standout."

There was a host of women who wouldn't agree with him. "Only a suggestion, but if you do something contemporary, you have a good chance to win the next competition."

"Think so?"

It was the same conversation she had with this man every month, and every month he did the same impersonations, and lost. As Ivy listened, she flipped the pages of her desk calendar to October, and tapped her pen on the date she'd circled in red. The date her balloon payment was due.

If she wasn't solvent by then, she'd promised to

give up her dream, and as her father said, "take a normal job, like a normal woman." When she'd agreed to these terms in exchange for help in financing, two years had seemed an eternity. How could Party Animal miss?

Decorating the shop and selecting the stock had been more fun than she'd ever had before, and the response of customers was gratifying. Before long, she projected, she'd have to hire a full-time helper. Then she'd have to go out and find a location for Party Animal #2.

People who came in were enthusiastic about her advice on menus and games. Her racks, they said, were filled with special cards and decorations they couldn't find anywhere else. So where were the crowds that word-of-mouth advertising was supposed to bring?

When the bell over the door jangled, she brushed her caller off as politely as she could, and prepared to greet the first customer of the day.

"May I help you?" She swallowed hard. It wasn't a customer. At least she didn't think Logan McKenna had come for help planning a party.

He was the last person she wanted to see. No; the last would be the representative from Intrigue Novelties, wanting to know why his check hadn't arrived.

Logan had left his jacket in the car. His shirt was gray oxford cloth, open at the collar. He wasn't wearing a tie now. His charcoal slacks settled smoothly over his long legs, and his hair had a slightly disheveled look. Ivy liked him better this way.

What was she thinking? She didn't like him at all.

He didn't say anything until his progress was impeded by the counter. "You aren't . . ." He looked past her, as if expecting to see someone else. "You can't be Ivy Canfield."

"I can be, and I am."

Her hair had been flyaway that morning when she got out of bed, as it always was when she'd been under stress. She'd brushed it furiously and twisted it into a shiny swirl atop her head. This swirl she'd fastened with a length of wide red ribbon, to match the hip-length red tunic she wore over forest green tights. It was the kind of festive outfit clerks in a party shop should wear, though she hadn't managed to convince Florence to cooperate.

"Are you all right?" he wanted to know.

"I told you I was."

"That's right. Fainting runs in your family."

His smile pulled an unplanned one from her. "I told you about that?" In her confused state she must have been jabbering. What other secrets had she disclosed? "How did you find me?"

"The manager at Smoothee-Freeze. He said Dandy was an employee of Party Animal and gave me your address. I couldn't find your phone number in the book."

"I'm in the white pages." Not missing the raised eyebrow, she added, "I'll take out an ad in the yellow pages when I'm on my feet."

His expression said he didn't think she ever would be. "You ran out on me."

He sounded as if such a thing had never happened to him before. ''When I tried to tell you I wasn't interested in a job, you wouldn't listen.''

''In your weakened condition, you couldn't be expected to know what was best for you.''

In the interest of heading off another argument, she decided to leave his statement unchallenged. ''So what brings you here?'' she asked, noticing with irritation that her heart had picked up a beat at his nearness.

''My reasons are threefold.''

Threefold? It wasn't a casual comment. He was sliding back into his stodgy identity. Good. That made him much more resistible.

''Do you want to start enumerating those reasons?'' ''Enumerate'' was a suitably stuffy word too, she thought.

''I felt called upon to check on the condition of the drenched little waif who lay shivering on my couch yesterday.''

''I was drenched because someone slapped a dripping rag on my head. I was shivering because you keep your office like the inside of an igloo.''

''You look fine.'' Another smile shimmered in his eyes, making her ponder her earlier position. While she was still definitely a mouth person, there was something to be said for electric green eyes too.

She held her arms out to her sides to demonstrate the excellent state of her health. ''What's your second reason for being here?''

''I wanted to talk to the owner of Party Animal

about subjecting helpless employees to intolerable conditions. But since you're the owner, what can I say?''

She held out her arms again.

"Why didn't you tell me you ran your own business?''

"Why didn't you listen when I tried to explain?''

"You weren't speaking very clearly.''

An answer also subject to question. Once he'd removed Dandy's head, her enunciation had been perfectly clear—hadn't it?

"What about reason number three?'' She waited.

He picked up one of the novelty pens that when turned one way showed a dog standing in a snowstorm, and when turned another, showed a cat. "Could we go somewhere for coffee? We need to talk.''

"We do?''

Getting together for coffee was reason number three? Had he been perceptive enough, after all, to recognize the woman behind the grungy appearance she'd presented in his office? Could he actually have been stirred by her? She straightened a pile of thank-you notes that didn't need straightening.

His lower lip slid forward in fetching contemplation, and he nodded.

"I can't leave in the middle of the day,'' she argued, with herself as well as Logan.

He glanced around the empty room. "Too many customers?''

"I never know when I might be swamped.''

Not commenting, he turned the pen over and allowed the snowflakes to fall on the cat. "You make a habit of not eating lunch?"

"I have a big breakfast. Then I eat here, when there's a break. Lunch is in a refrigerator in back of the shop." She jabbed her thumb in the general direction.

"Is there enough for two?"

She willed herself not to register the suspicion that was coiling inside her chest. Why would Mr. Big invite himself to lunch? "Do you want strawberry or banana?"

He thought for a minute. "Strawberry or banana—what?"

She raised the hinged part of the counter and led the way to the kitchen. Actually it was only a curtained-off portion of the long, narrow room, but it had a sink, a chrome-and-Formica dinette set, a pint-sized refrigerator, and a toaster oven.

She opened the refrigerator and removed two small cartons. "Yogurt. What flavor do you like?"

Logan's grimace made her laugh.

"It's good for you."

"So is tofu. But I've lived this long without trying it."

"Isn't that a narrow-minded attitude?"

"Darn right."

She opened an overhead cabinet and moved some jars. "I also have peanut butter."

"What kind of jelly?"

"No jelly."

"A peanut butter sandwich without jelly?" He worked his mouth as if he had already eaten the sandwich, and was having trouble swallowing.

"Canned peaches?" she tried. "No? Then you're out of luck."

"If you have coffee, I'll take that. Sugar. No cream."

While she set out the cups, he pulled out a chair, sat down, and studied the business card he'd carried from the counter. It was shocking pink with a line drawing she'd made of Dandy and Toodles the Poodle kicking up their heels. Though she was no artist, the end result wasn't bad.

"Party Animal," he read. "Catchy name. Maybe you should pick a location that's not so off the beaten track."

As if the thought had never occurred to her. "Smack in the middle of a McKenna & Howard mall, I suppose."

"Can't go wrong there."

"Except that the rents are way beyond what I'm prepared to pay. I'm on a budget." Surely he knew what a budget was. Or did he? The Eldorado he drove wasn't an economy car, and his clothes hadn't come from the racks at K Mart.

"The extra foot traffic makes up the difference in rent."

"Not according to my figures."

"It takes a good two years for a new business to break even."

"I allowed myself two years." Almost.

He looked at her over the rim of his cup. "Even then, four out of five new ventures fail."

Was he still pushing his filing job? "I'm the fifth in that group. The one who succeeds."

"I hope so." He glanced down at Spiffy, who'd rubbed against his legs and was now trying to find a comfortable spot under his chair. "Is this guy in costume, or is he the real thing?"

"Spiffy has no show business ambitions. I tried to persuade him to be docile and allow petting. That way I could take him to the Children's Hospital when we entertain."

"He won't cooperate?"

"He decides who has the privilege of his affections."

A crooked smile came and went. "He takes after you, then?"

"You could say that." Ivy cast narrow eyes at her guest.

"You leave him here, as a watch cat?"

"No way. He goes with me in the morning and back with me at night. He hates to be alone."

Logan took another drink of coffee. "Where are you from, Ivy?"

"You're not still trying to locate my guardians, are you?"

He grinned. "No. I was thinking that you might have better luck with this business if you started in your hometown, where everyone knows you."

She peeled the top off her yogurt carton and sat in the other chair. "You're assuming that I'm from a small town. I was born in St. Louis. We didn't move to Sedalia until I was twelve, when my father went into business for himself."

He nodded. "So why did you come back?"

"Partly because I wanted to be on my own." She didn't say anything about her need to escape her father's authority and constant presence.

"You said 'partly.' What's the rest of the story?"

"I love St. Louis. The sense of history everywhere I look. The Old Courthouse where the Dred Scott case was tried. The reminders of the World's Fair and the first ice-cream cone. The levee and the riverboats. All of it." She shrugged, wondering if she'd babbled too much. "Even though I haven't had time to see any of those things except at a distance since I came back."

"Too busy trying to keep your head above water?"

"And the sharks from snapping at my heels."

His laugh was rich and genuine. "You aren't alone. The weather is unpredictable here, and the years have taken their toll on the city itself. But oddly enough, St. Louis people always seem to consider themselves St. Louis people, no matter if they've moved to Houston or Salt Lake City."

He was friendly today, making it almost seem that she'd imagined the upright, uptight man who'd delivered an insulting lecture to her at the mall.

"Can't you remember what it was like when you were starting out in the business world?" She leaned toward him. "Didn't you take chances in the beginning?"

"Some chances have more disastrous results than others." Meaning he knew the difference, and had always acted with extreme wisdom.

"Maybe you had a wealthy family who cleared the way for you."

"No money in my family." He added another spoonful of sugar to his coffee. "I got my share of right crosses to the jaw before I realized I had to crawl before I tried to run."

It would have been easy to drop her guard when he was like this. But as he spoke, quietly and earnestly, she sensed there was something he wasn't saying. He was a man of purpose, and his purpose for being here wasn't to discuss the pros and cons of their chosen city.

She was almost afraid to ask. "You didn't tell me your third reason for paying me a visit."

"Yes. Well. We had a meeting," he told his coffee cup.

"Why do I wonder if Dandy was the subject of that meeting?"

"I'm afraid he was." He picked up the pen and turned it so the snow fell on the dog again. "The verdict was that Dandy isn't welcome at Toluca Woods anymore."

Chapter Four

As her spirits plummeted, Ivy controlled the impulse to dump the contents of her yogurt carton over Logan's head. She needed Toluca Woods. She'd counted on it, when she figured up how she could make her rent and add to the balloon payment fund. Without that mall, and others McKenna & Howard managed, she was lost.

"You're here under false pretenses." She snatched away his coffee cup and sprang to her feet.

"Ivy . . ."

"All that sweet talk and—and flirting."

His mouth dropped. "I was flirting?"

She held out one hand to restrain him, though he wasn't coming toward her. "Turning on that boyish, aw-shucks charm. Waiting for exactly the right moment to drop the bomb."

A car screeched into the curb. Rap music spilled from its open windows, making further conversation impossible.

When she'd decided on this location there had been a shoe store on one side and a mailing and lockbox business on the other. There was ample parking on both side streets. People doing business with these stores would notice her. It would only be a matter of time before she was up and running.

Actuality had been less positive. A month after she'd signed the lease, the city put signs up restricting parking, and the shoe store moved. The mailbox business remained, but many of its customers were loud-mouthed, seedy types who loitered around, crushing cigarettes on the sidewalk and leaving trash in the gutter. The owners didn't keep the parking strip mowed or their windows clean. The front needed paint badly, but her pep talk about an inviting exterior had been met with a "so-what" stare.

"You want I should scrub the sidewalks, lady? People come in to send packages. They don't care what color we paint our doors."

"You aren't going to cry, are you?" Logan asked, when she had put his cup in the sink, run water in it, and stood with her back to him for many long moments.

She arrowed her glare at his face. "Do I look as if I'm going to cry?"

"Frankly, yes. And what you call flirting was only an attempt to be helpful," he said, still smarting over her accusation.

" 'Could we have coffee together?' " She twisted her face in insulting imitation. " 'Wouldn't you be better off starting a business in your hometown?' Forget it, Mr. McKenna. I don't give up that easily."

"Like it or not, Ivy, on the road to success you'll run into barriers." He emphasized this universal truth with a sweeping gesture. The mouth she'd previously admired took on the maddeningly resigned expression mouths took on when the trouble being discussed affected someone else. "You'll either surmount these barriers, or you'll go under."

While she seethed in silence, he held forth about the myriad reasons for this action by his office. Traffic jams Dandy could cause at Toluca Woods. Insurance hikes. Children dashing between cars. Noise.

"Creating an atmosphere not conducive to comfortable business dealings."

"Are you finished?" she asked.

He scraped back his chair and stood. "I think I've covered everything."

"And then some. You've taken this unfair, and probably unconstitutional, stand because Dandy fainted."

"Unconstitutional?"

"Unconstitutional," she repeated, "and unwarranted."

"It was a decision reached by discussion with the tenants." He waited for the comment to sink in. "They agree that it's undignified being represented by a duck."

"Smoothee-Freeze can't have voted against me."

"The decision has to rest with the majority."

"Isn't that how dictatorships start? Crushing the rights of the individual for the good of the majority?"

"I presented the facts."

"The facts according to Logan McKenna."

The bell over the door jangled, and a woman with crimped white hair came in with a shopping cart she parked to the left of the counter. She smiled at Ivy and moved to the greeting card rack. Ivy smiled too, in spite of the rage that was spreading rapidly to all points inside her.

Logan was unperturbed. "In a city the size of St. Louis, you have countless shopping centers and strip malls. Places you can try to get your giant animals situated."

And McKenna & Howard controlled most of them.

"Could you help me, Miss?" the woman called. "I hate these modern cutesy cards. Don't you have something with birds and flowers? I need wrapping paper too, for a baby shower."

"All right, Mr. McKenna. You've presented the threefold reason for your visit," Ivy said tightly. "Go home. I have a customer."

"If there's anything I can do . . ."

Wasn't that what people always asked when they intended to do nothing at all?

"Miss . . ." the woman tried again.

"I'll be right with you," Ivy called.

When Logan reached the door, he looked back. "I don't have an argument with you, Ivy."

"That's what you think," she said under her breath. "Hold on. Don't move."

He waited as she strode toward him, a faint smile curving his lips, as if he imagined his teddy-bear countenance had won her over.

Confronting him, she plucked the cat/dog pen from his coat pocket with a flourish. "This is not yours," she said.

His mouth opened in his confusion. "I'm sorry. I automatically . . ."

"I'm sure you did," she said meaningfully, turning away.

Not until the bell jangled, signaling his retreat, did she allow herself to look back.

"He won the battle, but not the war," she fumed to herself. "My side only needs to regroup."

"Did you say something, dear?" the woman asked.

"Nothing." Ivy pasted on a smile. "Let me show you a shipment that just came in."

"So you're the gal responsible for the chaos in the parking lot the other day." The Ace Printing Shop proprietor put on his half-glasses to study the petition Ivy had handed him. "Heat got to you, did it? You gotta watch that midday sun. It can be a killer."

"It isn't something that happens every day," she explained, telling him about her need to take over the Dandy job when she wasn't prepared, and about her failure to eat breakfast that morning.

"I know the struggle it is to start your own business.'' The man scribbled his name on the line she indicated. ''The wolf was always at the door for the first five years when I started this place.''

Five years? Ivy questioned silently, after she'd thanked him for his cooperation and set off for the next shop. If it took her half that time, she'd be lost.

''I have no objections to pie-in-the-face presentation,'' the man at Superior Travel Agency said, when Ivy presented her case. ''Advertising's where it's at, and heck, we get the overflow from all the attention.''

''Exactly.''

''Sure, I'll sign.''

She'd done it. Her heart was racing with such gleeful satisfaction, she wanted to dance back to the van. The fabric shop, the last stop on her list, had been a harder sell than the others. The woman in charge had back problems that made her snappish at first. But in the end, she'd signed.

''I enjoy seeing a young woman making a success in this man's world,'' she said.

Not only had Ivy managed to get the seal of approval on Dandy from all the proprietors at Toluca Woods, she had an engagement at the flower shop the following month for the unicycle-riding mime on her roster of talent.

''What are you going to say now, Logan McKenna?'' she muttered later, as she dialed the business office at Toluca Woods.

To her disappointment, he wasn't in, and wasn't expected that afternoon.

"He'll be here from about eleven to one on Tuesday," the woman said.

"I can't wait that long." If she held the news inside much longer, she'd explode. "How can I reach him now?"

"Maybe you can catch him early tomorrow morning at Green Hills Center," the woman offered. "I'd advise you to make an appointment."

"Fat chance," Ivy said to herself as she hung up. Only an ambush would be effective with Mr. High-and-Mighty.

The next morning, dressed in a slim, celery-colored linen dress with a single strand of multicolor beads at her throat, she was already waiting in the underground parking lot when Logan's car swerved into an executive slot. This time he was carrying a briefcase. He wore a gray suit with a faint blue stripe, a pale blue shirt, and his usual pompous expression.

"I don't have time to argue with you, Ivy," he said, after doing a double take at her unexpected appearance.

"My visit is onefold," she teased, falling in step beside him.

Not smiling, and not slowing his pace, he bent his arm to look at his watch, though he probably knew what time it was to the second. "I have only a few minutes before an important meeting."

Not to be dissuaded, she trotted after him up the steps, across the entranceway, and into the building.

The furniture in this office was ultramodern, with white paneling and lots of brass.

When he settled behind his desk and began rummaging through drawers, she slapped the manila folder in front of him.

''What's this?''

''It speaks for itself.''

''It doesn't say a word to me.''

She hadn't noticed before, but the irises of his eyes were ringed with a deeper shade of green, making the lighter part more intense. She dragged her attention back to the petition and cleared her throat.

The phone rang, and he snatched it up, swiveling in his chair so that his back was turned. ''I'll have an answer for you by Thursday,'' he told the caller, then nodded, and nodded again, at what was being said. ''I'll get back to you as soon as possible.''

''You'll note that the approval of Dandy by your tenants was unanimous,'' Ivy said when he'd hung up. He swiveled his chair back, and she was able to look him in the eyes again.

His lower lip slid forward delectably. ''You don't take no for an answer, do you?'' Was there a touch of admiration in his tone?

''Supposedly, you were shutting Dandy out because of the will of the majority.'' She tapped a finger on the folder. ''There you have the decision of the majority.''

He stared at her. ''You walked into those shops with

that face, and wearing that dress. What man could have turned you down?''

You, evidently, she didn't say. ''I wore a simple tailored dress.''

''A simple dress is the worst kind on the right woman.''

He had a maddening way of giving a compliment and taking it away at the same time. ''What are you accusing me of now?''

''I'm saying you used a woman's subtle version of strong-arm tactics on my tenants.''

''Note, please.'' She tapped the page again. ''Half the signatures belong to women.''

His smug expression faded. He glanced down again, then up at her. ''I don't have time to discuss this now.''

''No need for discussion.'' She was taking a chance by antagonizing him, but her best strategy would be to insist on an answer before he had time to consider. ''Give me a simple yes, and I'll disappear.''

''Logan.'' A balding man in a plaid sport jacket looked in. ''They're in the conference room.''

''Thanks.'' Logan straightened his shoulders, yanked at the knot of his tie, and unfolded into a standing position. The appealing, indefinable scent he carried about with him wafted to her nostrils as he prepared to walk past her.

She moved into his path. ''Well?''

He glanced through the partly open door to the cor-

ridor, where the man in the plaid jacket waited.
"Okay, Ivy. Okay."

"Okay means yes?"

"It usually does, doesn't it?" He executed a small,
stiff bow.

She could barely keep herself from throwing herself
at him and giving him a hug. He would certainly have
misread her enthusiasm. Or maybe he wouldn't have.
"Thank you."

"With an 'if' tagged on." He held the door open,
and waited for her to go first.

She complied. "If?"

"If Dandy causes the slightest ripple in the routine
at Toluca Woods, he's out on his tail feathers. Is that
understood?"

"Understood."

"No unexpected visits like the one today. No fetching smile or tearful blue eyes will help him."

"I didn't suppose they would." Was he getting
back at her for accusing him of flirting?

His glance swept to her toes and back to her face
again, a smile glimmering in his eyes. "Didn't you?"

"I can't believe you plan to wear that duck suit
again." Florence dropped her books on the counter.
"Not after that fainting incident. Maybe you should
just let this assignment go."

"Toluca Woods is too important for Party Animal.
And there just isn't anyone else qualified available. I

58   *Virginia Hart*

can't take a chance. Dandy is on probation. One mis-
step and he's through. I have to do this, and do it
right." Ivy grinned. "Or you can, if you want to
volunteer."

Florence's guffaw made her glasses dance on the
silver chain she wore around her neck. "Can you see
me cavorting in a duck costume?"

"I'm leaving early to get a parking space close to
the mall. That way, I can dash to the van for a drink
when my throat is parched." Ivy straightened one leg,
then the other, wriggling into her yellow knit leggings.
"Besides, I took off four rows of feathers last night,
and added two air vents. The costume is cooler."

"I *thought* Dandy looked a little slimmer."

"Don't worry. I'll be fine."

Florence wasn't convinced. "I hope so."

The morning went smoothly with only two slight
hitches. A little girl's balloon popped, and she let out
a wail. Fortunately, Ivy was able to shape a replacement into another dachshund immediately. She dubbed
it "Elmer," and in seconds the child was giggling.

Self-congratulations were in order. The work she'd
done on her costume alleviated the problem of over-
heating. Even when the midday sun beat down, she
didn't feel any adverse effect.

The first problem popped up when she dug in her
box of tricks and discovered she had no more balloons.
It was okay, though. She had "Guess-What" bags left
over from a birthday party. Children always liked the

idea that no one knew what they'd be getting until they opened their bags. She only hoped the supply lasted through the day.

At two o'clock, she was about to retreat to the van for a break, when she felt a numbing pain as if something heavy had fallen on her left foot. Letting out a yelp, she peered through the slits of Dandy's eyes to see a boy of about six with orangey red curls, a smattering of freckles, and an impish grin. She recognized him as a child she'd seen a few minutes before when she handed him a grab bag.

Before the pain had eased enough for her to tell him that such behavior was out of line, he stamped on her other foot and laughed.

"Why did you do that?" she asked, in a quacking voice that helped hide her anger. Maybe she could win him over with reason, and send him on his way.

"I'm Patrick, and I want a Guess-What." He held out his hand.

"You already had one, Patrick," she said, through clenched teeth.

"My prize was a stupid paper umbrella. They're for girls. Give me another Guess-What."

"Come back tomorrow," she managed, hoping he wouldn't take her advice. "You can win something else."

"I want it now." With that he grasped her beak and yanked as hard as he could.

"Hey, that's enough."

He laughed and made another grab.

"Stop it right now. Just stop it." Holding out her hands to protect herself, she took several shuffling steps backward.

When she'd worked part-time for the Department of Parks and Recreation, she'd prided herself in her knack for winning mischievous children over, but that knack was severely cramped by being in costume. Dandy's next alteration would have to be a way to achieve better communication.

When the boy giggled and reached again, she thrust her arms through the air pockets she'd sewn in the duck's uniform, caught him by the shoulders and gave him a gentle shove. "Go find your mother."

At her touch, he let out a deafening shriek, as if he were in pain, and darted across the parking lot. "Mommy!"

There was a screech of brakes as a car skidded to avoid him, and a man yelled out the window. "What are you trying to do, kid, get yourself killed?"

Uneasily, Ivy glanced in both directions. Logan was nowhere to be seen. His car wasn't even in the lot. Fortunately no one came out of any of the shops, and the driver zoomed off without saying anything more. But all wasn't well. A slim brunette in a white linen jacket was heading toward her, with a triumphant Patrick in tow.

The woman wasn't glaring, however, and if she was the little boy's mother and dealt with him all day, she must have known that he could be difficult and unruly.

"Dandy," the woman said, in the ultra-reasonable

voice some people used with children. "Patrick has been a good boy all week. He'd like one of your grab bags, please."

Two other children sat at one of the umbrella-covered tables outside of Smoothee-Freeze watching the events with interest. Giving out extra treats to reward misbehavior would not only be unfair, it could start an unpleasant precedent.

"I'm sorry," Ivy said. "I already gave him one."

"She's a liar," Patrick yelled.

"Dandy is only mistaken, dear," the woman said too sweetly. "He sees so many children, he sometimes forgets when he's left one out."

"He already had a Guess-What," Ivy insisted, deciding not to mention that the boy had stamped on her foot. Something told her the woman wouldn't believe her. "He didn't like the prize, and threw it away."

"Liar," the boy bellowed, his face turning as red as his hair.

Fastening steely eyes on Dandy, the woman thrust a beautifully manicured hand into the grab bag. "Dandy will be glad to give you one, darling. It's his job, you see, to make boys and girls happy. Not to make them cry."

"I want Dandy to give it to me, not you." Snarling in fury, the boy slapped at the Guess-What the woman held out to him. It fell to the ground where he stamped on it, and raced across the parking lot again.

"Patrick, wait," the woman cried, giving chase.

Deciding that a vanishing act would be the best solution, Ivy put a DANDY WILL BE BACK SOON sign in the window, and hastened to the van, where she allowed herself ten minutes to cool off and drink a glass of orange juice.

One bad experience in two days wasn't bad, she reminded herself philosophically. By the time she took up her post again, doting mother and rambunctious child would likely be gone.

They were, and all was serene. She'd have to remember to add a note to her list of instructions for new employees, advising strategic retreat in case of trouble.

Chapter Five

The heat wave continued through the next five days, but Ivy didn't mind. She'd won back Toluca Woods, and victory was sweet. To make up for the inefficiency of the ancient air conditioner, Florence donated a standing fan from her apartment.

"At least it blows the hot air around," the woman said.

Business had picked up, due to flyers she'd had her part-time employee Scott put on cars in supermarket parking lots. She'd included a coupon offering 10 percent off, as well as free noisemakers with each five-dollar purchase.

She was able to pay outstanding bills, add a bit to her balloon payment fund, and work out an easy-pay plan with the novelty company.

Her mime had been hired for the opening of a used

car lot in South St. Louis, and Scott entertained at a birthday party in Ferguson. Reports on both were excellent and return performances were possible. To satisfy Florence, she'd hired a high school girl for "rush call" mall appearances. Though the girl could only work weekends, she was enthusiastic, and pronounced the idea of dressing up "a blast."

Then a real cause for celebration came in the mail. An invitation to the upcoming Convention of Small Business Owners, to be held in Kansas City. With it was a letter of proposal from the Convention Committee. Someone had heard about Party Animal.

Many members would be bringing their families. Some would have small children, and though child care would be provided at shared costs, the committee felt that it should offer entertainment.

If you can supply a magic act, the letter said, *as well as a clown, to wander the outdoor children's area every day from twelve to three, rooms will be furnished, along with expenses. If interested, please call for confirmation.*

If she was interested? Yes, yes, yes. This would be her first convention. Party Animal had arrived.

A quick phone call assured her that her magician, Martin the Magnificent, would be glad to get the work. Scott was enthusiastic too about taking Jingles the Clown on the road.

"One problem. I can't work the Sunday gig," he told her. "My sister's coming in from Texas. She'll only be here one day."

"It's okay," Ivy said, after a few moments of contemplation. She couldn't refuse this opportunity, and a clown outfit would be more comfortable to wear than Dandy's suit had been. "According to the convention itinerary, there isn't much scheduled for that time slot on Sunday. I'll play Jingles myself. If the costume fits."

"Can't hurt if it's a little baggy," Scott reassured her. "It'll only make you look more comical."

The call to Florence took a bit more wheedling. The woman wasn't crazy about working the extra days. Her feet hurt when she stood too long, and she needed time for studying.

"I'll do it this once so you can attend your convention," she finally agreed. "But you'd better start breaking that new girl in on the cash register."

It was raining by the time Ivy had checked her receipts, finished her phone calls, and was ready to go home. Good, she thought. A few sprinkles would cool the air and give a refreshing drink of water to the potted tomato plant on the balcony of her apartment.

Spiffy, eager to get back to his scratching post, was sprawled on the counter, now and then emitting a complaining meow.

As Ivy gathered the papers she planned to work on at home that night, a rattling at the front door caught her attention. "We're closed," she called, sprinting over to put her mouth to the crack in the door.

When the rattling came again, she yanked up the shade enough to see that her visitor was Logan. His hair was wet and his shoulders hunched against the downpour.

Surprised to see him, she opened the door, stretching a foot across the opening to keep Spiffy from making a dash. "Don't let the cat out."

"Spiffy," Logan acknowledged, as if he expected an answer from the would-be escapee, who'd leaped down ready to accept the challenge.

"I was about to leave." Ivy leaned down to open the door of the pet carrier.

"You told me you haven't been to the waterfront since you were a little girl." Logan hoisted the carrier onto the counter and held it steady while she stuck the struggling cat inside. "I thought you might like to go tonight. We could have dinner."

"You and me?" she questioned.

"I'm not inviting Dandy."

Now she was *really* surprised. At the very least, she thought he'd have been miffed by her going over his head to collect signatures from his tenants. Who would have guessed that Logan McKenna, a man she considered to be entirely self-engrossed, would remember what she'd told him about her love of the historic section of the city?

"Right now I have to meet a plane at Lambert. But I could pick you up at about eight o'clock." Taking her silence for assent, he ripped a sheet of paper from the notebook he kept in his jacket pocket. "Write your address down for me."

Laying the paper on the counter, she hesitated a few moments before beginning a rough map.

"I only asked for your address," he protested.

"Finding my apartment isn't that simple."

"Like Party Animal?"

Ignoring the crack about the inaccessibility of the shop, she began scribbling names of the streets, marking turns with arrows. "My neighborhood is a maze of dead ends. You have to be sure—"

"I'm an old hand at finding my way around town," he interrupted, plucking the paper from her hand. "All I need is your address."

"Don't say I didn't warn you."

As she locked up and turned the sign in the window to CLOSED, Logan carried Spiffy's carrier to the van. "Eight o'clock," he reminded her.

Maybe her luck really was changing, she thought, as she watched him drive away.

Putting aside her admitted attraction for the man— however unsuitable he might have been—going out with him would be good business. Here was the perfect chance for her to mention other shopping centers under his jurisdiction. Maybe—just maybe—over dinner, she could get Toodles the Poodle reinstated at the East Side Minimall too.

By eight o'clock, she'd changed both her hairdo and her dress twice. By eight-fifteen, she wished she had time to change back to the simple, black sheath dress she'd discarded earlier, deciding it was too sophisticated for a casual dinner date.

But was the summer cotton she'd chosen sophisticated enough? It was off-white, with a print of apricot butterflies. Would Logan think butterflies were schoolgirlish?

By eight-twenty, she'd taken off her charm bracelet and replaced it with one made up of simple gold links, deciding the echo of the enameled butterflies would be too much. By eight-thirty, she'd removed the combs she'd used to hold her hair back from her face, and allowed it to fall to her shoulders as it usually did, shiny and full of bounce.

By eight-forty, she'd taken off her shoes, propped her feet on the coffee table, and turned on the TV news, trying to be philosophical about being stood up.

As she was preparing to order a pepperoni pizza and call Ron perchance to share it with her, the doorbell rang.

"Sorry." Logan breezed in at five miles an hour. "The plane didn't arrive on schedule, and I didn't have your phone number to notify you I'd be late."

"No problem. Do you still want to go?" she asked lightly, as if she hadn't been stewing since the little hand of the clock pointed to the hour.

"Unless you've already eaten." He made a visual survey of her living room, taking note of Supergirl cape and mask she'd left on the window seat. He raised an eyebrow. "Is there something about you I should know?"

"It isn't mine." She laughed at his inference. "That is, I don't wear it. I'm getting stock ready for Halloween. Sometimes I sew at night when I watch TV."

"This early?"

"It's not nearly early enough." She stepped into her shoes, and fastened the narrow leather straps. "Halloween was always my favorite holiday when I was little. But the costumes in the stores were such a disappointment. Cheap taffeta that tore. Ties that broke, and witch costumes that no self-respecting witch would be caught dead in."

"I usually threw a sheet over my head and called myself a ghost," Logan said.

She smiled, not able to imagine Logan at any age hollering "trick or treat." "I order basic costumes from the catalog, and make them more realistic. Some I sew from scratch."

He twisted his mouth to one side. "You can't charge enough for a costume to make the labor worthwhile."

She decided not to question his stress on dollars and cents. "The ones I make, I'll rent, not sell. I won't have many ready for this Halloween, but in a year or two, I should have an entire line."

"Sounds to me as if you work around the clock. Are you sure that Supergirl outfit isn't yours?" he teased, opening the door and offering his arm.

Laclede's Landing was the only section of the city that remained from the original grids laid out in the mid-eighteenth century when St. Louis grew up around a French trading post. Close to the west bank of the Mississippi River, its charming old buildings, restored or being restored, were mostly brick, like the narrow streets. Here was a jarring mixture of old and new, with the gleaming band of the Arch rising 600-some feet above it all.

The rain that came and went without relieving the summer heat didn't discourage tourists, who were out in force taking advantage of the specialty shops and nightclubs, and adding a festive mood.

The restaurant Logan had chosen had either once been a riverboat, or had been fashioned to look as if it had been. A paddle wheel was fastened to the left of the heavy teakwood door and the entrance could be reached only by crossing a swaying ramp enclosed on both sides by thick ropes.

The theme continued inside with maps and charts on the wainscoted walls, along with anchors, pencil sketches of boats, and yellowed photographs of riverboat captains. Each of the tables held a flickering lantern and the dinner offerings were written in chalk on wooden boards.

The crispy-coated catfish and its tangy sauce were delicious, along with garlicky mashed potatoes and hot cornbread sticks.

As they ate, Logan told tales of his college days, about his liking for football, but how a broken leg had laid him up for most of the season. Summers after that, he'd spent learning the construction business, where he'd felt completely inept, and ended by falling off a ladder and breaking his other leg.

He wasn't as handsome as she'd supposed he was on that first day of their meeting, Ivy mused as she listened. It seemed so long ago. But then, she had been looking at him through Dandy's eyes.

His chin was firmer, and his eyes more deeply set. His nose was even a trifle crooked. From one of his football injuries? His crisp hair, the color of maple syrup, could be unruly, she imagined, and the natural dips and bends difficult to control.

Yet this man, whose laugh was infectious and booming when he wasn't throwing his weight around, whose compelling eyes changed shades according to what he was thinking, was far more attractive than she had imagined at first sight.

After taking various jobs—on a loading dock, at a trucking company, and in a dog kennel—he'd gone to work at a private airfield, and even thought for a time of becoming a pilot.

How smashing he would look in a pilot's uniform, she reflected. "But you don't fly anymore?"

"I haven't for a long time."

"I've always heard that once a person experiences the exhilaration of soaring through the clouds, he finds he can't give it up so easily."

Logan didn't elaborate, and quickly changed the subject, as if the conversation had opened a door in his memory better left locked.

At his urging, Ivy talked about how her father had

set a deadline, making her agree to come into the family business if she couldn't pull her shop out of the red by then.

"I'm putting some aside each week in a special account to cover the balloon payment." She didn't add that lately she'd had to dip into it to meet expenses.

"Why didn't you wait until you could arrange your own financing?"

"My father has friends in the banking business, and was able to arrange loan terms on his signature, without my knowledge."

"You might have guessed it wouldn't be that simple for someone who had no financial history."

Her father had said the same thing when she flew at him, furious, with what she'd discovered about his interference.

"Under ordinary circumstances that's true," she agreed. "But I already had money of my own, from an inheritance left by my grandmother. I believed that made me a good risk."

"If you lose the shop, and the inheritance is gone, your father wins."

She sighed. "Don't count me out yet."

Relaxed in each other's company, they took longer over their meal than would have been necessary. Ivy had already eaten too much, but the dessert cart held such a tempting array, she couldn't resist.

Besides, she didn't want to go home yet. As much as she had learned about Logan already, she knew there was more, much more. Her choice was a creamy apple concoction with flavored whipped cream and delicate shavings of chocolate across the top. Logan chose the same thing, but with strawberry filling instead, and they shared.

"My father is a generous man," she said when they were enjoying tiny cups of rich, strong coffee. Out of long habit and family pride, she didn't want Logan to judge her father too harshly. "He was doing what he thought was best for me. But he also likes to be in control."

"That's where you get your determination."

She bit off the protest before it reached her lips. Her mother was a quiet woman, content to remain in the background and allow decisions to be made for her. "Maybe that's why he and I bump heads so often."

"I gather you'd rather not work for him."

"I won't." She pierced his eyes with hers. "I intend to succeed."

"You might at that." His smile was boyish. "Do you mind some advice?"

"You'll give it anyway."

With seeming concentration, he smoothed out a wrinkle in the tablecloth. "Don't go out on jobs yourself."

"I don't." When he gave her a sideways look, she added, "The time you met Dandy was an emergency."

"Put all your efforts into making a success of the shop. Spend money for advertising. Forget Dandy and Doodles . . ."

"Toodles," she corrected.

"As it is, you're spreading yourself too thin."

"How?"

"People stop by, find you're not open, and don't bother coming back. I know from experience," he said, reading the question in her eyes. "It took me two trips to catch you."

"My clerk is going to summer school, and can't put in many hours."

"Exactly what I'm saying. Hire people who *will* be there."

"I can't afford to pay anyone full time." She didn't care for his know-it-all suggestions. It brought out an argumentative side of her own nature she didn't particularly like. "But thank you for your advice."

He raised an eyebrow. "Don't get defensive on me again, Ivy."

"You simply don't understand. I want more than just a shop where people buy wrapping paper and greeting cards."

"More in what way?"

"I want people to automatically think of Party Animal when they think of giving a party. *Any* kind of party. *Any* special occasion."

"Better practice your scales then, in case somebody wants a singing messenger."

"I don't sing."

"What if one of your emergencies arises?"

She sighed, realizing that the personal side of their exchange had all but evaporated. He was back to being all business again. "Then I'll have to pray the birthday boy or girl is tone-deaf."

He reached across the table to cover her hand with his. "You're lovely, Ivy. You're charming and vibrant, but you're also too soft."

"Too soft, why?"

"For the kind of operation you're considering, you have to be a take-charge type. You have to maintain dignity, so that clients know they can rely on you."

"Dignity," she repeated, wondering if he realized that his thumb was gently stroking the back of her hand, and more important, if he knew what it was doing to her.

"And you can't maintain dignity dressed in a duck suit. You have to be cool and calculating. You have to develop a killer instinct."

"I already have one."

"That, I'd like to see." He laughed, and signed the check the waiter had placed on the table. "Ready to go?"

Chapter Six

When they left the restaurant, they strolled along the levee, absorbing the smells and sounds of another era, aided by the lapping of the water, the cobblestones underfoot, and the chugging of the boats anchored along the way.

"I have a confession to make," Logan said sheepishly. "The plane wasn't delayed." When she looked at him, puzzled, he added, "I was late getting to your place because I got lost. I should have let you draw that map."

"Don't let it spoil your record." She bit back a giggle. "The UPS man has a hard time finding me too, when he has to deliver a package."

"The crew who laid out that street must have reinforced themselves with liquid refreshment first. I had to stop three times to ask directions. Nobody seemed to know.'' His fingers first touched, then twined with hers, warming her from her hairline to the soles of her feet.

''If you had given up and gone home, I would have forgiven you.''

''That, I wouldn't have done, if it took me until midnight.''

''Because you wanted my company?'' she couldn't resist asking. ''Or because you don't like to admit defeat?''

''A little of each. To make up for keeping you waiting so long, I'll take you on a excursion one night, if you'll let me,'' he said, as they came to a stop before the *Delta Queen* riverboat. ''There's an orchestra on board, and dancing.''

''I know. Our school scheduled its yearly picnics on a boat.'' She remembered the slapping of dark waters, the pulsing of the music, and her thoughts of Mark Twain, of Tom Sawyer and Huckleberry Finn. How much more she would enjoy it now, dancing in Logan's arms.

''Then you wouldn't want to go again.''

''Oh, but I would!'' Her stomach muscles contracted as she realized that she'd answered too quickly, and with too much enthusiasm.

He smiled, and her blood rushed through her veins like a mountain cataract. Somewhere at the edges of her consciousness she was aware of voices, and footsteps of tourists who milled around them, enjoying the night. It didn't matter. In her eyes, there was only she and Logan and the possibility that he might kiss her.

When it didn't happen after many long moments, with effort she wrenched her gaze to the tubular steel arches of the massive Eads Bridge above and to her left.

"They say twelve men were killed constructing this bridge," she said, needing to say something.

"I'll bet you know when it was built to the day."

"I know it was dedicated on July Fourth, 1874, in front of a crowd of fifty thousand people. I did a paper on it during my freshman year."

"With your leaning toward history, maybe you should have become a teacher."

"Instead of a duck?" she shot back. "As I believe I've said before, I like what I do."

His eyes rolled skyward in an expression of surrender. "No offense meant."

"None taken."

"I wonder."

"Maybe a little," she admitted.

"I don't want there to be any hard feelings between us," he said solemnly, looking down at her.

"There aren't any."

To her disappointment, he started to walk again, this time toward the parking lot. He'd brought her here with dinner in mind, not a romantic rendezvous, she was forced to admit. It was his way of conceding defeat at Toluca Woods, though it wasn't his style to congratulate her.

He liked her, she was almost sure. She couldn't have reacted to him so strongly if it hadn't been true. On the other hand, he was such a stickler for business, he probably thought it advisable to keep business and pleasure separate. Maybe he was right.

By now, traffic had thinned on the expressway and they were home before she was ready. Sensing that he planned to offer only his hand in saying good night, and overcome with an irresistible impulse born at the riverside, she rose on tiptoe and kissed him lightly on the lips. "Thank you for tonight."

Though she'd instigated the kiss, he took over. After a small play of features that signaled his surprise, he slid his arms around her, tightened them, and scalded her lips with his, giving her a rush of delight that drew the breath from her.

When he relaxed his hold, allowing her to sway dizzily from the effects, he kissed her again.

From somewhere far off she heard herself offering an invitation. "Would you like to come in for a cup of coffee?"

She didn't even have coffee. She'd forgotten to pick up a jar at the market that day. But it didn't matter. She only wanted to make the evening last.

"Not tonight."

Hadn't he said "not tonight"? That meant there would be another night, didn't it?

She smiled to herself as she fumbled in her handbag for the house key, hoping her fingers weren't trembling too badly for her to fit it in the lock. Inside the apartment, she could hear Spiffy mewing on the other side of the door, wondering why she hadn't come in to dish out the kibble.

"Wait." Logan's hands came to rest lightly on her shoulders.

He'd changed his mind? "Yes?"

"There's something I meant to tell you at the shop and couldn't. Then later, I didn't want to spoil . . . dinner and—everything that . . . happened later."

She'd never heard him stammer before, and it was endearing. She gazed up at him. "Yes?"

Why did he look so serious?

It occurred to her all at once—in the ensuing silence—and she knew exactly what he planned to say, and it wasn't endearing at all.

"There was a complaint about Dandy," she said for him.

"I'm afraid so."

Patrick and his mother. It had to be. Patrick had probably been the same child who'd caused trouble before too, and caused Brian to quit. He was one of a kind.

"One complaint," she said tightly. "From one woman whose little boy is completely out of control."

"He was so frightened he was nearly hit by a car trying to get away."

"He had a tantrum, and dashed out without looking."

"That's not the way I heard it."

"The driver was going twice as fast as he should have."

Logan laughed dryly, and leaned with one hand against the wall over her head, an out-of-place lock of hair falling over his forehead. If he had been feeling guilty before, those feelings had flown. "Why is it that Dandy's never at fault?"

She ignored his question. "Does this mean you're barring Dandy from Toluca Woods again?"

He nodded.

"Why did you waste a whole evening for both of us?"

"I don't consider the evening wasted," he said, so softly she almost didn't hear. Or maybe it was because of the rage pounding behind her eyes.

"That talk about no hard feelings. You knew you'd be getting your way. So why didn't you have one of your many secretaries dash off a letter?"

"I warned you, Ivy."

"You're being unfair."

"It's you who's being unfair. Who's at fault isn't the question here. It's my job to stop trouble before it starts."

"I suppose you thought that if you kissed me, I'd be too starry-eyed to care when you broke the news."

"You kissed me first, remember?"

"So you improvised." As she fumbled with her key, Logan attempted to take it, and unlock the door for her.

She wrested it away. "Surely you'll admit I can unlock a door for myself, even if you don't think I have the brains to run a business."

"I never said that." He caught her wrist. "You don't have the necessary experience to run a successful business."

"Go," she said, pushing him with her free hand.

"Ivy, we need to discuss this."

"You and your discussions. *Go,*" she said louder.

No wonder he'd tried to persuade her to put Dandy on hold and concentrate on running the shop. That was why he was stressing the need for dignity, and suggesting that she return to Sedalia and start where people knew her.

He didn't care if she opened in Iceland—in fact, he'd prefer it.

Now she was glad she hadn't told him about the offer from the convention committee, and the Sunday she'd be dressing in a clown costume to replace Scott. He'd only roll his eyes and say that it was exactly what he would have expected from her.

The door across the hall from her apartment creaked opened, and the elderly woman, who always spoke to her when they met, peered out. "Is everything all right, Ivy?" She glared at Logan.

"Fine, thank you. I'm sorry we disturbed you. Mr. McKenna was just leaving."

Logan returned the woman's glare, then turned it on Ivy. Growling deep in his throat, he strode off, almost tripping over the stones that surrounded a flower bed in his haste.

Spiffy's sympathetic meow didn't do much to dispel

Ivy's sense of being used, but finally she stooped to pick up the little cat anyway. Why had Logan choreographed tonight? Did he enjoy the sense of power it gave him to lift her to the clouds, then drop her down to earth?

She squeezed her eyes shut, and tried to take comfort in the little cat's contented purr. After a brief moment, she opened them again—wide.

"McKenna & Howard," she said slowly.

She'd heard McKenna's decision, but how about Howard?

She wasn't licked yet.

After a night of sleeping on it, she felt even more optimistic about going over Logan's head again. She could only hope that his partner would be more reasonable.

"I have an appointment with Theo Howard," Ivy told the receptionist.

"Ms. Canfield?" The woman ran a finger down a list in front of her. "Go right in. The last door at the end of the hall."

When Ivy saw the woman seated behind the desk, she almost did an about face. Theo R. Howard was female? Slim and cool, she had a cap of glistening black curls and eyes that looked silver in the artificial light. She wore a gray silk suit and the same stiff smile she'd worn when she demanded that Ivy give dear Patrick another Guess-What bag.

"I'm Thea Howard. What can I do for you?"

Thea—not Theo. How could she have made that mistake?

Though she'd carefully rehearsed her speech, Ivy wondered if she should bother. "I imagine you already know why I'm here. I was hoping I could convince you to give Party Animal's services another chance."

"I'm afraid not." The woman clasped her hands on the desk in front of her. An opal ring glittered on the third finger of her left hand. "Is there anything else?"

"We didn't meet under the best of circumstances." Ivy tried for a chatty tone. "I wanted to apologize for the misunderstanding."

"Was that all it was? A misunderstanding?"

"I believe so. And I believe too that we can straighten it out. I've brought brochures explaining what we have to offer the merchants at Toluca Woods."

"I'm surprised."

"Oh?" Was that good or bad?

"Logan said he'd already dealt with you." The woman's expression didn't change. "But then, he can be such a softy. I'm not so easily persuaded. That's why he and I make such an effective team."

Logan, a softy? It was hardly a description Ivy would have used. "Dandy is very good with children. We've never had a problem before."

"If I recall, there was a similar instance when you lost your temper, and forgot you were a lady." Thea made a tsk-tsk sound with her tongue. "As I see it, your service isn't suitable to the quiet business atmosphere we try to maintain at Toluca Woods. Your giant duck would be far better dealing with a rowdy group. Such as those you'd find at a pizza parlor, or the opening of a—a discount department store."

"Dandy is always well received wherever he goes."

"He might work at birthday parties too," the woman went on. "That is, if you can take a bit of friendly advice."

Ivy felt her toes curling inside her shoes. "What might that be?"

"Go to the local college. Take courses on child psychology. You should learn how to deal with the public if you're going to continue in your line of work."

It was practically the same thing Logan had said to her. Obviously the two had compared notes. Silently, Ivy recited the first verse of "Little Bo Peep," trying for control. "Maybe you're the one who should learn about child care."

The woman's eyes narrowed. "What do you mean by that exactly?"

"I don't deny that Patrick's cute, but he's about as spoiled a child as I've seen."

Thea looked at the telephone for a long moment, before turning her attention to Ivy again. "Patrick is mature for his years."

"Mature? Is that what you call it when he stamped on my foot and tried to tear my costume?"

"I don't believe he did those things."

"You'll admit that he screamed at the top of his lungs and tore across the parking lot without waiting to see if a car was coming?"

"It was only because you frightened him. So badly, in fact, he had a nightmare that night. I was up most of the night with him."

"If you think he was frightened, you don't know your son as well as you think you do."

"If your plan was to make points with me, Ms. Canfield, you're going about it all wrong, attacking my son—someone who's too young to defend himself." The woman took a deep breath. "My husband was killed in a small plane crash when Patrick was only a year old. It hasn't been easy raising him alone, but I believe I've done a good job. At the same time, I worked hard and made a success of my life without asking for any handouts."

Did the death of her husband have anything to do with Logan's unwillingness to talk about his own flying days? Ivy wondered.

Maybe Thea had achieved success in business without help, and maybe she hadn't. Maybe Logan had been there for her. Was there more to their partnership than just a business?

"I'm not asking for handouts," Ivy said.

"Aren't you?" The woman's stare turned glassy. She rose, and crossed to the door. "I doubt that there's any reason to continue this discussion, don't you?"

Ivy tucked her brochures back in her satchel, and rose too. ''Yes, I do.''

''Don't imagine we're barring you from Toluca Woods, dear.'' Thea offered a cool, smooth hand. ''Come back any time you like—as a customer.''

Chapter Seven

In the days that followed, Ivy kept busy, struggling through the worry of losing a large chunk of income, as well as the pain she felt at Logan's treachery.

She attended a revival of *Hello, Dolly* with Ron, and to a performance of the St. Louis Symphony Orchestra. Though she kept a cheerful face for his sake, the evenings were wasted as far as she was concerned.

She came home from the concert to find that Logan had phoned three times. She played the messages over, then over again, sitting on the couch, pressing a pillow to her chin. His words were brief, and colored by characteristic impatience.

"Ivy, if you're there, pick up."

By now, he knew about her meeting with Thea. Maybe he'd known it all along. She had no intention of returning this call, or of answering any of his future ones.

But she needn't have worried. The week passed, and she didn't hear from him again. As far as he was concerned, it was over. His conscience was clear.

At last, convention week arrived, and she was ready for it. The hotel was elegant and beautiful, with sweeping panoramic windows, glistening chandeliers, and plush carpet muting the sounds of activity. It was conveniently located, but not in the main snarl of the business district. Built some distance back from the street, it was screened from traffic by potted shrubs and a stand of poplars.

Martin the Magnificent and Jingles the Clown, alias Scott, had arrived ahead of schedule and were already settled in their rooms.

Ivy was settled too, in far more luxurious quarters than she'd expected as an employee, in one of the cottages behind the main hotel. She had cable television, though she was sure she'd have no use for it, and an enormous bed. The carpet was like lush green grass underfoot, and the walls were a lemony yellow, making her think of a sunlit morning.

There was even a refrigerator stocked with bottles of apple juice and sparkling water. From one of her windows she could see a serene pond complete with water lilies, and a fountain with the marble statue of a serving maid pouring water into a basin.

From the other, she could see a rose garden, with a

sundial inscribed with the Browning quotation that said the "best is yet to be." She certainly hoped it was true.

She'd already spoken with the man in charge, who'd been pleasant, helpful, and concerned about their accommodations. Breakfast was a delicious buffet, with herb-flavored sausages, butter croissants, and fresh strawberries. Lunch was even better. The orientation meeting was exciting, and she looked forward to the afternoon session.

Now she had to check the bulletin board and see if she had time to dash back to her room to freshen up before she went to the next meeting.

"It can't be!" She groaned, then glanced around the hotel lobby to see if anyone had heard her reaction to the information posted.

They hadn't. There was too much first-day bustle.

She might have known that there would be a snake in the grass.

Logan McKenna.

Logan was one of the scheduled speakers. His topic: The Alternate Approach in Redevelopment.

Why hadn't she noted his name on the itinerary? Would she have given up her opportunity to attend the conference if she had? No. In fact, when she thought about it, she welcomed the chance to hear what he had to say, as long as he didn't find out that she was in the committee's employ, or for that matter, even present. She had no intention of allowing him to snicker at Jingles the Clown, the way he had at Dandy.

But how would he find out? So many people were in attendance, he couldn't possibly notice one insignificant member of his audience. Especially if she took a seat in the back of the room. Considering how busy he was, he wouldn't stay the whole four days. He'd offer his wisdom to the teeming masses and depart.

The first speaker, a florid man who kept wiping his forehead with his handkerchief, spoke about meeting dynamics. Ivy gleaned a number of useful tips and jotted them in her notebook. Who could tell? Before long she might have enough employees to need advice on company meetings.

The second speaker, an attractive woman with short gray hair, presented charts showing the upswing of the economy in the last five years and the exciting opportunities for the small business owner with imagination and spunk.

Dashing in a dark blue suit, Logan took the stand next. The smoothness of his delivery spoke of his having made many speeches on the same subject. Yet he managed to maintain enthusiasm.

All over the auditorium, pens scratched as he made points. Now and then a flashbulb exploded.

"Hah," Ivy muttered in spite of herself, when he compared renters in the malls to families helping one another over rough spots, tolerating little irritations, making concessions.

"Mr. McKenna," a woman called, after he'd recognized her with a pointed finger during the question-and-answer period. "Don't you mourn the loss of neighborhood shoe stores and dress shops?"

"Change always brings a degree of sadness. Look at the market for nostalgia nowadays. I'm no different, and I'd like to be able to say that single businesses will stay healthy. But look around you."

"Dinosaur," a man in an Hawaiian shirt grunted, glaring at the woman who'd expressed her negative opinion. "Scared to death of progress."

"Think of what's happened too many times in the past," Logan continued. "A mom-and-pop hardware store in business for twenty years is suddenly squeezed out when one of the big boys moves next to it. That can't happen with our kind of unity. The job of management is to see that two businesses aren't pitted against each other in the same center."

More questions were raised, but all Logan's answers were slanted to make malls seem idyllic.

Forgetting her desire for anonymity, Ivy sprang up. "Unfortunately, Mr. McKenna, the management in these malls you call families, don't recognize individuality."

Logan shaded his eyes with one hand. If her unexpected appearance jarred him, it didn't show. "Miss Canfield?"

"If one merchant wants to paint his window boxes yellow and plant pansies," she went on, "a vote has to be taken by the committee to see if it will be allowed."

"That's right," someone across the room agreed.

"Aren't family decisions arrived at in the same way? With compromise?" Logan answered.

"Not in *my* family," another man said with a snort, and everyone laughed.

"As your malls spring up," Ivy said, feeling encouraged by the support, "the rights of the few continue to be sacrificed to the will of the strongest."

"That's true everywhere," Logan admitted. "What about political elections? The candidate who gets the most votes takes office."

"Usually the candidate that can afford the best advertising," someone said.

"The malls offer tenants that advertising," was Logan's answer.

"As long as those tenants conform to a long list of petty rules," Ivy argued.

"You got that right," a man in the front row said. "My daughter came home from college. I said she could sleep in back of our shop for a couple of days till she got settled. Somebody found out, and boom, one of your committee members showed up with a warning that it had better not happen again."

"You gotta move with the times, if you're gonna survive," the man in the Hawaiian shirt grunted, louder this time.

"Don't you miss the days of being able to walk through the business district of a town and shop at one store and then another at your leisure?" Ivy asked.

"I do," a woman in the first row said. "Sometimes I feel like I'm on a treadmill."

"Better a treadmill than having to hop in your car and drive from one store to the other, fighting traffic and hunting for a place to park,'' came an answer from the other side of the room, followed by a smattering of applause.

''As far as I'm concerned,'' Ivy said, ''the fact that we've given up our freedom of choice cancels out the benefits.''

More scattered applause followed.

Because of her heated involvement, the discussion went overtime, with people all over the auditorium contributing opinions. Later, when the crowd began to circulate, she had almost as many people gathered around her as Logan did. Now and then she caught his eye, and he didn't appear to be pleased by the competition.

When the time was up, though butterflies still fluttered in her middle from the confrontation, the worst was over, she decided. She was glad she'd stood up to Logan. He'd be on his way home, and she could enjoy the remainder of the convention in peace.

The conference room assigned to the next session was huge, but tables had been set in conversational semi-circles. By now Ivy knew many of the faces, and even the names that went with those faces.

At first, when the woman in charge asked members to stand up and contribute to the proceedings with a short presentation about his or her business, Ivy had no intention of speaking out. But after a number of others had shared their experiences—good and bad— she thought, *''Why not?''* What point was there to a gathering like this unless everyone took part?

As the rest had done, she told briefly about how Party Animal came to be. About how even as a small child, she'd loved giving parties, even if her guests were her dolls. She talked about her stint in business college, where she picked up the basics, and the job she'd held at the Y that started her dreaming about a business that would allow her to work with children.

"I love what I do," she said, preparing to wind up and allow someone else a turn. "Maybe because running a party shop allows me to remain a child myself."

"Wouldn't it have been more practical," came a resonant male voice from a table in the middle section of the room, "if you'd paid your dues by taking a job in retailing before jumping into your own shop with both feet?"

She didn't have to seek out the source of the question. She knew Logan's voice well by now.

"Did I forget to mention that I also worked in a five-and-ten-cent store when I was in high school?"

"Waiting on customers doesn't provide the kind of experience I meant."

"Have you ever worked at a five-and-dime?" she shot back, feeling heat building in her face and neck. "Unless you have, you can't begin to understand how valuable it can be in learning to deal with the public."

"Ain't that the truth," someone said. "You meet all kinds."

"But it doesn't teach you about merchandising or inventory," Logan said.

"He's right on the money there. It takes time to learn to analyze the buying habits of the public," a woman next to Ivy agreed.

"And always keeping a reserve," added someone else, "for replenishing stock that's sold out, and buying big-time on an item that's hot."

"But not buying *too* big-time," the woman added. "That's where a big percent of beginners fail."

"I'm extremely careful how I spend money," Ivy assured them. "The best direction, I've found, is to stock a large variety, to offer customers a choice, but not too much of each item."

"But without experience under the cloak of a company that knows what it's doing," Logan insisted, "mistakes are unavoidable, and mistakes can be deadly."

As before, as she and Logan batted the subject back and forth, others joined in, and the discussion turned lively, until the woman in charge announced the next contributor.

Making a point not to look in his direction, Ivy sat listening politely, trying not to let her simmering anger show. How petty it had been of him to retaliate for what he'd probably considered her attack in the auditorium by undermining her talk. Evidently he wasn't used to having his advice questioned.

When the meeting was over, and the announcement came that dinner would be served in the Garden Room, she decided to forgo the evening meal, and slip away. The day had been a full one, and she didn't want to chance running into Logan again.

The air was sweet with summer flowers and the night sky was peppered with stars. Instead of going directly to her room, she'd take the path through the rose garden and enjoy the night. When she heard footsteps behind her, double-time, she didn't have to turn around to guess that it was Logan at her heels.

''Bad strategy to withdraw now,'' he said, catching up to her.

''Why?'' she asked.

''People want to know if you're professional enough to rise above our difference of opinions.''

''Does it matter what they think?''

''It must, or you wouldn't be here.''

He was right. Those in attendance were fellow shopkeepers and possible future customers. Why allow anyone to believe that she'd been intimidated?

''So we kiss and make up?'' she threw at him.

''First things first.'' A smile shimmered in his eyes. ''Dinner's being served. Why don't we sit together?''

''You think that's necessary?''

''Definitely.'' His fingers curved around her elbow, and he led her back the way she had come.

''I don't think I like being under scrutiny.''

''If that's the case, you shouldn't have spoken out.''

''What you said about mall families was too outrageous to ignore.''

''And what you were saying about the ease of starting your own shop was too naive.''

''You were only trying to protect the others from my illogical logic then. You weren't trying to get back at me.''

He looked genuinely surprised. "That's what this week is all about. Most of us who've attended these gatherings before make a point of dropping by various groups and injecting a challenge to shake things up."

"So it was pure chance that we attended the same meeting."

"Not at all. I saw you go in, and wanted to hear what you had to say."

"What made you think I'd say anything?"

He tapped a finger to his forehead. "I know you fairly well. It isn't in your nature to sit quietly and let everyone else talk."

"Maybe not," she admitted.

"On the other hand, you did get under my skin in the auditorium. You tried to pin my ears back."

"I think I succeeded part of the time."

"I think you did too," he admitted, leading her down an aisle of tables set with white cloths, gleaming silver, and candles in etched glass globes. He pulled out a chair. "But I know I'm right. Unfortunately we can't roll the calendar back to horse-and-buggy days."

"Why did I know you were going to say that?" His grin was maddeningly attractive, and she had to work to remember how he'd misused his charm before. "How are you enjoying the convention so far?"

"It's exciting. I hope I won't miss too much when . . ." She broke off, deciding not to say that Sunday she'd have to skip some scheduled events because she'd be blowing up balloons for the children in attendance.

Why verify his opinion of her faltering financial status by confessing that she was here on a working holiday? That in a way, she was singing for her supper?

"Coming to the convention was a wise move on your part," he said, apparently not noticing that she hadn't completed her thought.

"You're actually crediting me with wisdom?"

"You have your moments," he teased. "Anyway, you'll make a lot of contacts."

"I have already. My dresser top is covered with business cards, and I've given out dozens of my own."

"Ever been to Kansas City before?

"Not for a long time."

"It has a lot to offer. I can show you the sights."

As he'd offered to take her on a moonlight excursion before he pulled the rug out from under her? "I don't think so. The itinerary will keep me busy."

"Not so. They've allowed breaks so people can swim, play golf, and see the city."

"Isn't that a waste of time?"

"Not at all. Solid meetings, one after the other, can be grueling even for the most enthusiastic participant. It's necessary to get off somewhere to brush away the cobwebs. So how about it, if for no other reason than to show you that I'm not a complete ogre?"

Why should he care? She could have accused him of not looking past his partner's accusations against Dandy. Of taking the easy way out by banishing Party Animal without regard to the consequences for her.

"Aren't you driving home tonight, now that your speech is over?"

"I'm here for the whole five days. Some people I need to see, I only run into at these conferences."

"But no more speeches?"

"No more speeches. So you can hold your ammunition."

"Will you promise to do the same, if I feel called upon to express an opinion at an upcoming group?"

"I'll try."

"Mind if we sit here?" A heavyset woman in a purple knit pantsuit sat next to Logan.

Her companion, a man with a camera around his neck, sat beside Ivy, and offered his hand. "Good to meet you two," he said. "We're from Springfield."

"St. Louis," Ivy said.

The two owned several pet stores and were thinking about franchise. They had attended the earlier discussion and to Logan's obvious discomfort, took over the conversation, putting so many questions to him, he hardly had time to put his fork in his mouth. After taking a picture of Ivy and Logan, the man handed Logan the camera and asked him to take shots of him and his wife.

When Logan's beeper went off, and he had to excuse himself to make a phone call, he looked ludicrously relieved.

With dinner over, people began milling around and dividing into groups. Ivy decided to skip the entertainment in the lounge, and escape before Logan came back.

"Don't go yet, honey," the woman coaxed. "It's early. Your boyfriend will be back in a minute."

Her boyfriend. Ivy wondered how Logan would react to that honored title. "Thanks, but I need to decipher my notes while I can still read them."

As she moved farther and farther away from the music and voices, she slowed her pace. With Logan out of sight, she was able to more easily balance her desire to spend time with him, against the reason for his impulsive offer to take her sight-seeing. Since he was stuck in Kansas City for a few days, he wanted someone to help him pass the time—preferably someone who would look at him, in the goofy, ego-feeding way she probably looked at him when they were together.

Well, he could forget it.

After she'd showered and dressed for bed, though, she found herself staring at the swaying shadows on the ceiling, part of her wishing she'd said yes to his invitation. How would she ever fall sleep? she wondered. But she did, almost at once.

Chapter Eight

Shallow pools in sunken places in the ground and on fallen leaves, as well as a clean, washed smell in the air, said that it had rained during the night, but there was no sign of it now.

The morning seminars—Establishing Recognition through Slogans and Logos, and Daring New Marketing Strategy—were informative, and started her brainstorming on her own.

After lunch, she caught sight of Logan with a group of other men, all carrying golf clubs. He was wearing a white polo shirt that exposed muscled forearms that would have drawn a second and third look even if he'd been a stranger. As she watched him, feeling safe at a distance, he spied her, raised a hand in recognition, and she almost dropped her handbag.

Reminding herself that a kiss or two did not a

forever-after romance make, no matter how giddy they had made her feel, she looked at her watch and saw that she had time to check on her clown. She'd already seen the magician take a quarter out of a little girl's ear to the delight of his audience.

Surrounded and scrambled over by giggling little ones, Scott was doing fine too.

"I'm having more fun than the kids," he said, in his Jingles the Clown voice.

"You'll be a hard act to follow," she told him, feeling stage fright at the prospect of taking his place on Sunday.

"You'll be fantastic. Be sure to use the spirit gum though, or your nose'll never stay on with these wild little ones."

Satisfied that the two young men were doing their job, now she had to get busy with hers and stop thinking about Logan.

One of her tablemates at the afternoon session was involved with the River Festival in Booneville, and thought a couple of Ivy's critters would be just the ticket to add excitement for the children. Then he introduced her to a woman from the Bluegrass Pickin' Celebration in September, who wanted to know if she had a hillbilly clown on her roster.

Ivy answered in an enthusiastic affirmative, assuring herself that it wasn't a fib. By September, she'd have a hillbilly clown, or whatever else a client might need, all lined up.

Since the bluegrass woman had suggested they get

together later, Ivy wasn't surprised at the knock on her door at about midnight, as she was getting ready for bed. Time meant little to many of the convention merrymakers.

Grateful for the business, she felt guilty about wondering briefly if she should pretend she wasn't home. She'd just showered and her hair was wet. After wriggling into her kimono, she peered through the side of the curtain before opening the door, and her blood turned to ice.

"I got through early and saw your light," Logan said through the gap between door frame and burglar chain. "Want to join me for a bite to eat? I hate to eat alone."

"The dining room is closed."

"I know a place."

She touched a hand to her middle, thinking of the huge buffet dinner she'd attended only a few hours ago, and the promise she'd made, as she piled her plate high, to make up for the indulgence by eating Spartan fare the rest of the week.

On another level, she wanted to be with him.

"I'll have you back by one-thirty." He held up one hand as if he were being sworn in as a witness.

"Wait till I get dressed." Had there been any doubt that she'd go with him, and at least keep him company?

Leaving him outside the door, she pulled on a pair of white chinos and a daffodil yellow blouse. After brushing her hair into a sleek ponytail, she took two extra minutes for a brush of mascara and some lip gloss. A pair of sneakers, and she was ready.

"Hard day?" It was a foolish question in light of the weary expression on his face. A lock of dark hair fell fetchingly over his glistening forehead. His shirt collar was open, and his tie was tucked in his jacket pocket. Where had he gone after the golf game that meant wearing a suit?

"Moderately."

"Did you win the game?"

"What? Win, and lose the account?"

"Sensible businessmen are that childish about winning?"

"I couldn't afford to take a chance. But I put up a good show." He swung a nonexistent golf club to demonstrate.

A White Castle sandwich shop was only a few blocks away, and though under other circumstances Ivy would have been tempted by her favorite chain restaurant hamburgers with their soft rolls and mounds of fried onions, she couldn't eat a bite. As he ate with gusto and she sipped a 7-Up, he talked about his family.

His father had once been a heavy drinker. His mother, a teetotaler at the time of their marriage, began to drink with him, to keep him company. In the end, the elder McKenna managed to quit, but by then, his wife couldn't stop.

"Reformed drinkers have no patience with those who still hit the bottle." Logan spooned chili on his hamburger with a lavish hand. "He walked out."

Devastated, his mother began to drink more and more. Logan had to take care of his two little sisters, seeing to their meals, dressing them, getting them off to school.

"It forced me to grow up quickly," he admitted. He held up his sandwich. "I wouldn't be able to guess how many of these things my sisters and I ate in those days, along with canned spaghetti."

"Do you see your father now?"

"Not often. He remarried and has two more children. My half brothers. They're good kids."

"And your mother?"

"I'm proud of her." He smiled. "When I was in college, she joined Alcoholics Anonymous. She was afraid she wouldn't be well enough to see me graduate otherwise."

"A happy ending to the story?"

He nodded. "She's married to a college professor, and living in Indianapolis. I fly there for Christmas, and on her birthday."

"I drive over to see my family at special times too. My father's birthday is coming up next month, but with this trip, I'm not sure I should take the time off."

On the way home, she told him about the friendly people she'd met at the hotel, and he talked about sights she should see while she was here.

"If sight-seeing doesn't appeal to you, we can rent

a boat, go out on the lake, and think about absolutely nothing while we drift.''

''Aren't you too busy to consider an idle day?''

''My day is yours, if you want it. As for tomorrow's sessions, the first talk is on mail order, and the next is called Franchising—Is It for You? I doubt you'd find much interest in either topic.''

''That's true.''

''Then there's a break. I'll have you back in plenty of time for when things stir up again.'' He held up one hand to show her his watch. ''One-thirty. I keep my promises.''

''It looks more like two-thirty,'' she corrected.

''It's the light out here.'' He grinned and dropped his arm. ''How did this happen? I meet a young woman in a duck suit, who's doing her best to create havoc in one of my malls. I drag her to my office to talk sense into her, and end up not being able to think about anything but her.''

A breeze ruffled wisps of Ivy's hair that had come loose from the elastic band, and Logan smoothed them into place. Somewhere far off a woman laughed. A car engine started.

''We don't know each other,'' Ivy reminded him, reminding herself at the same time.

''By the time the convention is over, we will,'' he promised.

''We've only been together . . .'' She couldn't re- member. ''A—a few times. We're a mismatch.''

When she stepped onto the landing, her eyes were

almost level with his. The trick was to say good night and slide through the door before he had time to take her in his arms—if that was his plan.

Or worse, before she had time to reach for *him*.

She'd forgotten to click on the outside light when she left, and his face, shadowed by a giant wisteria, was unreadable. But yes, he was going to kiss her, she was sure of it. She was also sure that if he did, she was going to kiss him back.

Suddenly, a question that had been gnawing at the corners of her mind struck. "How did you know where to find me tonight?"

"My cottage is next to yours."

She eyed him narrowly. "Why do I doubt that it was a coincidence?"

"Because you're the suspicious type?"

"I'm beginning to be."

"Okay. When I discovered you were here, I arranged for a room next to yours."

"Why?"

"How do I answer that?"

"With the truth?" she suggested.

"The lady wants the truth," he told the marble serving maid, who was still pouring water into the fountain. "All right. Here goes. I've thought a lot about you since our last dinner together. More than I like to admit. Is there anything wrong with that?"

"I suppose not."

"Then . . ." He broke off and only looked down at her.

It was time to go in. Standing with him in the moon-light was no wiser than it had been to start her own business without experience.

"You shouldn't have taken it on yourself to book a room next to mine," she said, clutching at something that might give rise to a disagreement.

"Why shouldn't I have?"

"I don't like people arranging my life for me. It was . . ." she began, then stopped, not able to find of the word she wanted.

"Yes?"

She envisioned herself pushing him away, and finishing her admonition about people making decisions for her. "It was officious."

"I apologize." When he leaned toward her, she tilted her chin to meet him halfway, and what began as a gentle good night kiss zigzagged to her toes and back again. When it was over, they clung together for many long moments without speaking.

"Don't forget," he said, kissing the top of her head before he began backing away, "if we're going to do everything we want to do, tomorrow has to start at sunrise."

Forget? she marveled. Did he actually thnk she could?

As she dressed for bed, she moved almost as if she were floating, grateful to the committee all over again for bringing her here, and visualizing a good-morning kiss from Logan.

They'd have breakfast together in the hotel dining

room before they started their drive. Or would he rather forget the morning meal, and stop on the way? It didn't matter, as long as they were together.

The telephone rang just as she'd dropped off to sleep.

"Sorry to wake you, but something came up," Logan said apologetically. "I'm afraid I'll be busy tomorrow after all."

Busy. She tried not to sound petulant as she thought of the plans that would be spoiled. "Will it take the whole day?"

"Probably. I'll try to get back for dinner. Save a place for me at the table."

"I will," she said, forcing brightness into her tone.

It was true what she'd said earlier. She hardly knew Logan McKenna, and much of what she knew didn't sit well with her. When had she become so possessive? And worse, how could his absence for a single day make her feel abandoned?

Chapter Nine

The bluegrass woman and the pet shop couple Ivy had met on the first night sat at the breakfast table with her. After the morning meetings, she accompanied their group on a bus tour to the Country Club Plaza.

Then it was the Liberty Memorial and several museums, all at a quick pace that didn't allow for musing. During the afternoon coffee break, she called Florence and learned that all was well.

"The shop is still here," the woman said.

"Did you call the card company about that short shipment we received?"

"Oops. It slipped my mind. Our algebra class is concentrating on exponents, and it's got me crazy. Sorry. I'll make the call immediately when I hang up."

"How's Spiffy?"

"He struts around my apartment like he owns the joint." Florence cleared her throat. "I don't remember school being this hard. After the mental beating I'm taken, I have a new respect for today's kids."

"Maybe you should have signed up for easy subjects first."

"Kiddo, I've been out of school for twenty-three years. Nothing is easy for me."

"I have to go now." Ivy saw one of her newfound friends beckoning. "They're returning to the platform. Good luck."

The first speaker was an impeccably dressed woman in her sixties who owned Nicholson Industries, a company that had candy stores all over the Midwest. The woman's story, about how she and her sister began in her kitchen, was funny and inspiring.

"Half the time," she went on, "after buying necessary ingredients, we had no money left over for groceries. We ate divinity for breakfast and chocolate nougats for dinner."

Finding herself next to the woman at the buffet table later, Ivy complimented her on her talk, and brought up the subject of Party Animal.

"It sounds like a perfectly lovely idea," the woman said brightly. "Where are you located?"

"In St. Louis. But our giant animals travel just about anywhere in the state, if a job involves more than one or two days."

"Our main office is in St. Louis too. Give me a call sometime next week." She handed Ivy a business card. "I know we can do business."

As exciting as meeting Clarice Nicholson had been, Ivy found that only half her mind was on the conversation. Logan had said he'd try to make it for dinner, but there was no sign of him.

He was good for her, she mused. How long had she put her mind this strongly on anything but business? How long had it been since she'd thought of anything but proving herself to her father?

When the meetings were over for the night, the others urged her to join them in the Topaz Room.

"They're having a South American shindig," the pet store man said, shaking imaginary maracas and executing a vigorous samba.

"I think they'll even form a conga line," his wife added. "Come on. It'll be fun."

"Thanks," Ivy said, "but I need to put my notes in order." *Not to mention my thoughts,* she added silently. It was possible that Logan would show up at her door as he had before, and she didn't want to miss him.

"If you change your mind, join us later. Wait a minute." The woman rummaged in her handbag, and brought out a snapshot. It was the one she had taken of Ivy and Logan at the banquet table. "You might like to keep this."

Though Ivy had meant it when she told them she

wanted to work, she couldn't. The four walls seemed to close in around her. Time and again, she found herself looking at the picture the woman had given her.

Though both she and Logan had smiled on command, his smile looked more like a grimace, as if he would have liked to strangle the one behind the camera, and Ivy couldn't help laughing.

She might as well face it. He wasn't going to be able to get away tonight. So why should she sit around her room moping?

After changing into a sleeveless summer dress in a riotous print that looked somewhat South American, she brushed her hair, put on lipstick, and set off for the Topaz Room.

Though the music had been lively as she came down the path, now it was dreamy and romantic. A contralto in a black velvet dress was singing Spanish lyrics to "You Belong to My Heart."

Not wanting to blunder into the dimly lit room, Ivy stood in the doorway, looking over the crowd. Colored lanterns had been strung everywhere, and the musicians, as well as the waiters, wore ruffled satin shirts. Was that her friends' table? she wondered, standing as tall as she could to see. No.

They weren't on the dance floor either. As she gazed over the couples that swayed in the dim light, with speckles of color like starlight swirling over their heads, she inhaled sharply.

There was Logan, achingly handsome in a charcoal suit. The striking brunette in his arms was Thea. She wore a white halter-neck dress with a wraparound skirt. A sprinkle of sequins across the bodice caught the light and made her sparkle.

When Logan said something close to her ear, she laughed, and buried her face in his shoulder.

Why should I feel so devastated? she tried to reason, as she flung herself from the ballroom. *Thea is beautiful and they're partners. Why I should I be surprised that they're involved?*

She'd cautioned herself from the beginning not to read too much into his spending time with her. Now Thea had arrived. Why should he bother with an ordinary shopgirl?

She bit her lip. So Thea Howard was the urgent business Logan couldn't cancel. Why hadn't he said so? Why did he have to lie?

Dazedly, she showered and dressed for bed, trying not to think. When she slid between the sheets, she willed herself to sleep, but it didn't work this time.

She got up once for a drink of water, and again to splash cool water in her face. Unused to sleeping in an air-conditioned room, she tried to open the window, but couldn't. When she turned the air-conditioned off, it was stuffy.

At one-thirty-six, according to the clock, she heard a shuffle of footsteps, and muted voices—a man and a woman—outside the cottage next door. The man said something in a low rumble, and the woman answered. Then the man said something again.

Metal scraped metal as the key searched for the lock. A door opened.

Ivy clicked the tableside radio on low. Then she pulled her sheet around her ears and fell asleep from sheer exhaustion.

Groggy from her restless night, and not at all hungry, she ordered breakfast at the counter, instead of in the dining room, where she would have to put on a cheery front.

"What are you doing up so early?" Logan asked, sliding onto the stool next to her, as if they could start up where they'd left off. He was wearing a navy-and-white T-shirt and shorts.

"I could ask you the same thing." She struggled to sound offhand. "Was your business successful last night?"

"Fairly." He ordered coffee and a cheese Danish. "That blouse and skirt look very businesslike."

"Thank you. I think."

"But I expected to see you in shorts or dungarees, wearing no lipstick, and your skin slathered with sun-tan lotion. We had plans, remember?"

She took a sip of orange juice to keep from reacting to his ridiculous remark in light of what she'd seen. What was wrong? Was Thea unavailable? "If we had plans, they were tentative ones, and I didn't agree to them."

"We were going to rent a boat and go out on the lake." He looked serious. "I told you, nobody follows the itinerary to the letter. It makes for convention burnout."

"Then who are all the people at the meetings?"

"Not the same people at all the meetings, if you notice. You're suppose to pick and choose what suits you."

"Why didn't I read that anywhere in my schedule?"

"It's a secret you learn after a while."

She made her eyes wide and round. "Then I'm getting the benefits of your years of experience?"

A puzzled look crossed his face briefly, as if he'd expected a more enthusiastic reception. "You could say that."

She studied the plate in front of her, wondering how long she could keep up the banter. "While conventions might be old hat to you, they're new and exciting to me."

His Danish arrived, and he began buttering it. "You're not particularly interested in tax shelters, are you?"

"I plan to be in the future."

"Or New Software that Runs the Business for You?"

"I keep up with what's new in computer programming."

"You don't have a computer."

"I'll get one—eventually." She picked up the pitcher of hot maple syrup and poured some on her French toast.

"In the meantime, how about that boat ride?" His face glowed with expectant victory. How could she refuse such a prize? And maybe she wouldn't.

If he had a hidden agenda, so could she. In the two or three hours they would be together, she could surely sneak in comments about the shop and how harmless Dandy was when given half a chance. With the open sky, the fragrant air, and a few warm breezes, he might be susceptible to brainwashing.

"You don't have any urgent business today?" she asked, stressing the word "urgent."

"Nope." He raised an eyebrow. "Some sweet tooth you have there."

She looked down to see that she'd poured so much syrup, it threatened to run over the rim of her plate. "Oh." She set the pitcher right and closed the lid. "It came out faster than I realized."

He shoved her plate back. "You can't eat that. We'll stop for a bite on the road."

"On the road? Sounds like you envision quite a trip."

"I do," he agreed.

"Uncle Logan!" squealed a small voice, and Patrick burst through the door, almost knocking a tray out of a waiter's hand.

Thea followed, wearing a white sheath dress with a turquoise chiffon scarf at the throat. "Good morning, Early Birds." She smiled at Ivy as if they were dear friends. "I called your room, Logan, but you didn't answer. Now I know why."

"Mom and I are gonna eat breakfast with you. I want pancakes." Patrick leaped onto the stool next to Logan, and leaned across to look at Ivy's plate. "Wow! See how much syrup she takes."

"It was an accident," Ivy said, feeling called upon to explain.

"Could we move into a booth?" Thea glanced around for a vacant one.

Ivy didn't say anything, but she had no intention of being part of their breakfast club.

"We won't be here long enough for that." Logan turned the stool around to face the aisle. "I'm taking Ivy boating."

"How nice." Though the words were pronounced with a lilt and Thea's smile was wide, Ivy heard something else. Could it have been jealousy?

"Awesome. I wanna go too." Patrick bounced up and down. "Uncle Logan, take me too. I haven't been in a boat a long, long time."

"I took you a few weeks ago."

"A few weeks is a long time. Please?"

"Why don't you two go without me?" Ivy broke in, seeing an excuse to escape. "I told some friends I'd have lunch with them."

"So have dinner with them instead," Logan said. "We'll be back by late this afternoon."

"Can I go, huh?" Patrick persisted.

"I've already arranged a sitter for you," Thea said slowly, clearly wanting to be persuaded otherwise. "She might take you swimming, if you ask nicely."

"I want to go on the boat with Uncle Logan and Ivy."

Thea sighed. "Darling, Ivy doesn't want to spend the day looking after a little boy."

"It isn't that," Ivy tried.

"Really? Then it's all right?" Thea turned a brilliant smile on Logan. "Patrick can be a handful. I wouldn't want to spoil your time."

Ivy didn't know what to say. If she refused, the woman would think it was because she didn't care for children. That was a reputation she couldn't afford, since she was in a business that dealt with them.

Besides, it wasn't true. She might have liked Patrick if she could get him away from his doting mother, who satisfied his every whim.

"I'll cancel the sitter then," Thea said. "And oh, Logan, there's something else. Those agreements have to be delivered to Otto Kingsley."

"I thought you were driving them over."

"Are you joking? I have two appointments this afternoon. Why don't you drop them on your way to the lake?"

Undecided, Logan looked at Ivy over his coffee cup.

"How long can it take?" Thea continued. "You only have to explain the new clause and get Kingsley's signature. Besides, he prefers doing business with men. According to him, women should be in the kitchen making gingerbread."

"I'm not luring Ivy away from business, only to make her sit through more of it," Logan argued.

"Leave her and Patrick at the playground next to the shore. They can watch the boats while you're gone."

Ivy took another sip of orange juice, though there wasn't a mouthful left in the glass. If she didn't know better, she'd think Thea had planned this ahead of time, wanting to be sure she and Logan didn't have time alone together. Maybe she hoped Patrick's behavior would drive another wedge between them.

"Do you know how to play War, Ivy?" Patrick broke in.

"Yes, but . . ."

"Good." Thea tried to give her son a kiss, but he squirmed out of her grasp. "Good-bye, young man. Have fun. And Logan, be back by five. There's a conference call coming from Chicago at the company suite."

Ivy sighed as she watched the woman walk away. How had this happened? At least with the exuberant little boy along, she wouldn't fall prey to Mr. McKenna's charms again. "I'll have to change my clothes."

"Hop to it then," Logan said. "We'll wait here."

Back at her room, she swept her hair up at the sides, allowed the back to fall straight to her shoulders, and fashioned a fluff of bangs across her forehead. As Logan and Patrick were both wearing shorts, she dug hers out too. The only pair she'd brought were white tailored ones she paired with a lavender-and-white knit shirt.

Once or twice, she questioned her mirror image about her plans and wondered if she should have someone take a message to Logan that she'd changed her mind. But in the end, fifteen minutes later, she was back in the coffee shop, ready to go.

It was a perfect day for boating, though swarms of picnickers had the same idea, and there was a waiting list at the rental yard.

"I've signed up, and I'm sure our name won't come up before I get back," Logan promised, settling Ivy and Patrick at a picnic table near a sandy area. "Thea was right. You two will enjoy yourselves better here than you would sitting in a stuffy library, smelling the old man's pipe."

"Phew." Patrick held his nose.

"Is that okay with you, Ivy?" Logan wanted to know.

"Fine." What else could she say?

"He'll probably be gone about ten years," Patrick said, as soon as Logan was out of sight. "Mr. Kingsley talks, and talks, and talks, and talks." He fell on the ground, and pretended to be unconscious from boredom.

"It doesn't matter," she said, laughing at his antics. "We can watch the boats."

"Who wants to watch? I wanna swim."

"You didn't bring a bathing suit."

"It's under my clothes."

"Well, I didn't bring one, and you can't go in the water by yourself."

"Your shorts are like a bathing suit. Come on."

"Okay," she agreed, remembering how hard it had

been when she was little, and was stuck with grown-ups who wouldn't let her go in the water alone, and wouldn't go with her.

"Awesome! I'm a good swimmer," he said.

"I'm sure you are. But stay close to the shore."

With a sigh, she trailed him, taking a beach chair to the shallow end of the water that was roped off for children and nonswimmers. She might have known Patrick would do exactly as he pleased. What pleased him was splashing ahead, and ducking under the guard rope to the other side.

"Great." Dropping her bag on her chair, she raced through the water to where he was waving at her. "Patrick, come back here!" she cried.

"I told you I was a good swimmer." He moved out still farther, and tread water. "Let's race to the other end."

"No. I want you back where you belong," she insisted, as sternly as she could. "Patrick!"

Ignoring her plea, he began to swim.

How did I let myself get talked into this? she wondered, swimming after him furiously.

"See, I'm a better swimmer than you." He climbed over the rope again to wait for her. "You kick your feet too much. You should let Uncle Logan teach you. He taught Mommy."

It figured. "Can we go back and play cards now?"

"Are you tired already?" he asked.

"Exhausted."

"Will you play War and let me shuffle?"

"Anything you want," she gasped, trying to get her breath. Now she only wanted to get away from the water, where it was safe.

Neither of them had brought towels, so they rented them at the window. Fortunately, no one had picked up her discarded handbag, and she still had her wallet.

"You look funny," Patrick said, giggling. He pointed at her. "Your hair's like a scarecrow's, all stringy and sticking out. Mommy's hair gets curly when it's wet."

"I'm not your mommy." She groaned when she realized that in her haste to get ready, she hadn't brought a comb or brush.

"Put a rubber band around it and get it out of your eyes so we can play cards," Patrick suggested.

"I don't have any rubber bands."

"I do." He dug in his canvas bag and pulled out a dozen *Star Wars* action figures, a rubber frog, a zippered sweatshirt with a hood, and a ball of string, before he located the rubber bands, wrapped around a deck of cards. "Hurry up. I want to play a bunch of games before Uncle Logan gets back."

"You said he'd be gone about ten years," she reminded him.

"Maybe he won't. You put the stuff back in my bag," he ordered. "I'll deal the cards."

"You took it out, you put it back," Ivy said firmly, not intending to be bossed around by a pint-sized male too.

He scowled, but did as he was told, probably in the interest of getting on with the game.

He was surprisingly expert at shuffling for someone so young. But it wasn't surprising when he kept attempting to slip cards with larger denominations out of his discard pile and back in the hand he held.

Ivy was an expert too at putting a stop to such tactics. In her baby-sitting days, many of her young charges had pulled the same stunt. In spite of the fact that she didn't let them get by with anything, they were usually happy when she came on the job again.

"Put the eight of clubs back, Patrick."

"I didn't use it yet," he whined.

"Put it back if you want to continue playing."

He scowled again, but after a moment of indecision, while he tried to decide if he could intimidate her, he did as he was told. "I didn't mean to put that one down," he said later, when Ivy's queen won in a war against his ten.

She lay a hand over his to keep him from retrieving the card. "Leave it."

"I don't want to use it now."

"Once you discard, you can't pick it up again."

"Who says?"

"The rules."

"Who made up those stupid rules?" he snarled.

"The person who invented the game, I guess."

She won the first and the second rounds. Since it was a game of pure chance, either player had an equal chance, so she saw no reason to throw things his way.

He thrust out his lower lip. "Mommy always lets me win," he growled, sinking down in his chair.

So he was smart enough to know that he was being humored. Ivy had to smile. "Do you like it when she lets you win?"

"I want to win."

"But if somebody lets you win, you aren't really winning. That can't be fun."

Patrick wrinkled his nose. "Let's play one more time."

It took two more games before he finally won, and when she groaned in defeat, he laughed so hard, he almost fell off his chair.

Ivy had to laugh too. "Doesn't it feel good to really and truly win?"

"What's going on?" Logan's shadow fell across the table.

"I won!" Patrick squealed, jumping up and down.

Logan shook his head. "I never saw him so excited about winning before."

"I really and truly won, Uncle Logan."

"Good for you."

"Ivy can't swim very good. She swims like this." Waving his arms in circles, he threw himself on the ground and kicked his feet frantically. "Will you teach her?"

"Whenever she's ready."

"Now?" Patrick asked.

"No, we'll have our boat in a few minutes." Logan grinned at Ivy. "So you went swimming."

"Not by choice, believe me."

He nodded, still grinning. "I believe you. Patrick can be persuasive."

"Tell me about it," she said, under her breath.

They bought fried chicken and potato salad at one of the stands, along with lemonade, and when their turn came up, took it with them on the boat. As he had on the drive here, Patrick monopolized the conversation, telling pointless knock-knock jokes, insisting on being allowed to steer, then asking questions about the birds on the water, about the people on the other boats, and about when they could come again.

"Again?" Logan ruffled his hair. "Forget about next time. Enjoy it now."

"When are we coming again, though?" He pointed at Ivy. "Will *she* come along too?"

"I don't know, buddy. She might have other plans."

"Will you?" The boy moved over to sit next to her.

"We'll see," she said, knowing in her heart that she should never have come along this time. That this would be her first and last outing with Logan McKenna.

Chapter Ten

As the boat nosed gently through the water, sending out ripples on all sides, Logan maneuvered a path around the other crafts. Ivy sat in the chair beside him with her feet up, and doing absolutely nothing. Patrick busily lined up his action figures on the floor for conflict. After much booming and banging, cheers, and war cries, all was quiet.

"He's asleep," Ivy said, looking over her shoulder to see the boy curled up on one of the deck pads, his eyes closed, breathing evenly. "He's really adorable."

"When he's asleep, you mean?" Logan chuckled.

"So you're aware that Patrick the Lovable sometimes transforms himself into Patrick the Terrible?"

This time he didn't take offense, as she suspected he might. "He's a bit spoiled. But why shouldn't he be? He never even knew his father."

"He has you."

"I try to make it up to him."

"Maybe you and Thea shouldn't bow to his every whim. It isn't good for him."

He gave her a hard look. "Why isn't it?"

"Because life isn't like that. Sometimes he'll lose and he'll have to accept it."

"There'll be time to think about losing when he's older. Now I get a kick out of seeing him happy." As the boat continued on its way, with Logan's hand barely touching the wheel, he began to talk about Patrick's father and the plane crash that had killed him.

Logan and Patrick, Sr., had gone to school together. When Logan got a job at the airfield, and learned to fly, he convinced his friend to learn too. At first, Pat refused. He liked his feet firmly on the ground.

"But he was a natural. Once he got a taste of it, he was always in the air. When things went wrong, it helped him unwind. When things went right, it was the ideal way to celebrate. Finally he bought his own plane."

He could get places faster, he told Thea, who balked at the extravagance, and refused to set foot in the plane. It beat commercial airlines, having to make reservations, and waiting for flights.

Logan looked up at the sky, his brows knit as he remembered, his stirring face sharp in profile. "Patrick was less than a year old when it happened. His father was returning from a business trip in Jeff City. The cause of the crash was never determined."

Logan had supposed he'd regret inviting Thea to take over her husband's end of the business. What did she know about any of it? But he hoped it would take her mind off her loss, and she accepted.

"Darned if she didn't turn out to be better with people than Pat, who could be a hothead."

"Was your friend's death the reason you don't fly anymore?" Ivy asked, deciding to bring it out in the open.

"Partly, I'd have to admit. It brings back too many memories. But then, I never took to the skies the way Pat did."

"I saw you and Thea last night," she blurted out, surprising herself with her own candor.

Logan waited, as if he expected more to her comment.

"You were dancing."

"Thea can't resist Latin American music. She lived in Argentina for eight years when she was a child and it got into her blood. We heard stains of 'Amor' as we were working, and she lost her concentration. There was no point in continuing. We didn't want to wake Patrick or the nanny, so we went to my room afterward, and stayed up half the night finishing our work. We didn't disturb you, did we?"

"I didn't hear you." That much was true. She'd heard nothing once they were inside his room. "Your urgent business was with Thea then?"

"Not exactly. A client flew in from St. Louis on the same plane. I had to pick them up at the airport, and the day went on from there."

"You dance well together." She knew she was pushing, but couldn't stop until she knew the whole story. "How long have you known each other?"

If he resented her questions, it didn't show. "Her father owned the airfield where I worked. She was my girl when I was in college."

"I see." From the way they'd looked on the dance floor together, executing smooth steps that spoke of much practice, Ivy would guess that Thea was still his girl.

"I took one look at her, and lost my head. She gravitates to certain colors. Since Pat's death, she wears mostly white and black. But in those days everything was red. Shoes, coats, scarves. Even her car. When she walked down the street, heads turned."

Ivy nodded, feeling a rawness at the back of her throat, as she heard the admiration in his voice.

"Then I introduced her to Pat." He shook his head. "Big mistake."

"How so?"

"They fell in love. Don't let anybody tell you there's no such thing as love at first sight. I'm a witness to it. From the beginning, it was as if nobody in the world existed except the two of them."

She knew the feeling. "You were brokenhearted."

"To put it mildly." He allowed his hand to slide around the wheel, hardly thinking about what he was doing. "It was a volatile relationship though."

"Volatile, how?"

"They fought constantly. And I use the word

'fought' literally. They screamed, slammed doors, threw things. Seconds afterward, they were back in each other's arms more inseparable than before.'' Logan shook his head. "It was odd too, because neither of them were like that when they were apart. I guess they brought out the best and the worst in each other.''

Ivy nodded, thinking that although she and Logan weren't so noisy about it, they were always at odds too.

''Watching them through that turmoil was more exhausting to their friends than it was to them. I made up my mind it would never happen to me.''

''Falling in love?'' Her voice emerged more breathy than she would have liked.

''Kissing one minute, screaming the next. It isn't the way to live.''

He looked long and hard at Ivy, and she looked away, wondering if he was reminding himself that because of their differences, she could never be a part of his life.

''It was after one of those heated battles that Pat was killed. It tore Thea to pieces.''

''How terrible for her.''

''Yes. It was more than the loss. She felt responsible, because they'd been quarreling bitterly when he left, and she said things she regretted. She wished they hadn't parted on that note. She's accepted that now. But for those first couple of years, I tried to be there for her as well as for Patrick.''

He still was, Ivy thought. And now, Pat Howard

was no longer standing between them. Was Thea ready to pick up where she and Logan had left off?

Another boat filled with teenagers, and traveling at top speed, zoomed past, too close, its radio blaring. Startled, Ivy sat up straight. "Should they be going so fast?"

"Someone will come out and put a stop to it."

"Before anybody gets hurt, I hope."

Logan glanced around, as if he'd been so caught up in thinking about Thea, he'd only now noticed that they weren't alone on the water. "Too many people here today. But there'll be other times for us."

Would there be? Not if Thea had anything to say about it.

"I'm fine," Ivy said. "You were right about taking time out to relax."

"At least you don't have to smile and make conversation with people who irritate you. Or dash from one room to the other according to a timetable. Sit back, close your eyes. Relax."

"You keep saying that," she said sleepily, feeling more content after his explanation of the previous night. "Are you trying to hypnotize me?"

"Not a bad idea." He maneuvered the boat into a small inlet, protected from the sun by branches of a low-hanging tree, and cut the motor. "You've been a city girl all of your life. That means you don't know how to let go."

"Sedalia isn't exactly a booming metropolis. And when did you live anywhere but in the city?"

He leaned back too, his hands laced behind his head. "There's a place I know, only a little over an hour's drive from the city. After a day or two there, with only the sky, the water, and a few birds, you forget you've ever seen a spreadsheet or a telephone."

"It sounds wonderful." Ivy's gaze brushed the canopy of willow branches overhead and remained. With the leaves so fresh a green, the sky so bright a blue, the brief stabs of sunlight that fell on her face and arms so cheery, it felt as if nothing could ever happen to change the closeness she felt to Logan now. "But I've never felt the need to escape."

"Yes, you have. You just don't recognize it yet."

"The answer to the ills of city living is to get off by yourself?"

"Better yet, with select company." Slowly he leaned toward her as if drawn by something beyond his contol.

"With a handful of your best friends?" she asked.

His lips were only an inch away now and his breath was steamy against her mouth. "Just one friend."

The first kiss was sweet and languorous, comforting in its familiarity, yet tantalizing in its difference. The second lasted longer and was more spellbinding, though neither touched the other with anything but their lips.

"Ha-ha! You guys think I'm asleep," Patrick piped up, suddenly standing between them, his eyes squinty with a wide grin. "I saw you kissing. Are you gonna get married?"

Ivy laughed, along with Logan. "When people kiss it doesn't necessarily mean they're going to get married."

"What does it mean?" the boy asked.

"It means they care about each other," Logan said.

Did he care about her? Ivy wondered, or was it only an invention for the little boy's sake?

Patrick climbed onto the rungs of Logan's chair. "But if you do get married, would she be my aunt?"

"I guess she would be, buddy," Logan said.

"Let's take the boat in. I'm getting seasick."

"We aren't moving. How can you be seasick?"

"Okay, I'm not seasick. But I'm hungry."

"We'll have dinner when we get to the hotel," Logan promised, looking at Ivy for confirmation.

For the ride back, Patrick insisted that Ivy sit in the back seat with him, so they could play strings. It took her a few minutes to remember the childhood game, but soon they were trading the string he'd dug from his satchel around his hand, then hers, then his again, making new designs with each exchange. After a few trades back and forth, the string got twisted, and laughing, they started again.

They pulled into their parking space at the hotel lot barely in time for Logan to return Patrick to his nanny, and prepare for his meeting. Ivy had to shower and change too for that evening's talks on Establishing

Customer Loyalty and Making Your Own Weaknesses Work for You.

As she was about to step in the shower, the phone rang.

It was Logan. "What about lunch tomorrow?" he asked.

"Lunch." She almost agreed enthusiastically, before she remembered. Tomorrow at noon she'd be prancing around in a clown suit. "I'm already booked for lunch."

"Should I be jealous?"

"You can, if you want to be."

"Hmm. I'll be tied up for dinner." He paused. "Then what do you think about taking a passenger on Monday morning when you head back to St. Louis? I'll spell you on the driving."

What did she think? Couldn't he guess? "What about your own car?" She clutched at her kimono as if he were in the room with her, and knew what she was thinking.

"No problem. I'll have someone drive it back for me. That way we can stop along the way whenever we feel like it."

Not until later, when she was combed and dressed and had almost reached the conference room, did it strike her. She believed Logan's explanation about Thea and the dancing. But would Thea's description of their evening together be the same? Had her desire to go dancing overwhelmed her only because she loved Latin American music?

Ivy didn't think so. She'd seen something more in the woman's eyes that morning in the coffee shop. Something that assured Ivy that she'd already made her claim on Logan and intended to defend it.

Enough, she scolded herself, impatiently shooing away negative thoughts. It was her, after all, not Thea, who would be riding back to St. Louis with him on Monday morning.

After breakfast on a tray in her room the next morning, dressed in her red polka-dot suit with bells on her cuffs, and her peaked hat, she leaned forward to inspect her clown makeup in the mirror. Not bad for her first time. Scott was right. The spirit gum held the rubber ball that was her nose so firmly it might have been her own. A good once-over with talcum powder set the white greasepaint, and she was ready.

Opening the door a crack, she peered in both directions. When she was sure the coast was clear, she dropped her room key in the pocket of her costume, and sped off.

Ouch. She hadn't gone far when she heard a familiar voice. Ahead, on the path, was Logan, talking on his cellular phone. He hadn't spotted her yet, but he was heading directly toward her at a brisk clip.

Retreat wasn't an option. He was moving too fast and she couldn't cover much ground in Jingles's floppy shoes. If she kept going, they would come face-to-face, and he would know the truth about her reasons for being here.

Hastily parting the shrubbery, she crawled through and arranged the branches in place.

"We'll discuss this when I get back. You have the material," Logan was saying.

Her breathing shallow, Ivy hunkered down, wriggling her real nose under her fake one to discourage a giant grasshopper who sat perched almost eye to eye with her.

"I can't do that." Logan stopped less than four feet away. "The contracts are signed."

"Eesh." She gasped involuntarily as the grasshopper leaped onto her shoulder. All she needed was for it to slide inside her suit. Brushing at it lightly, she sent it safely on its way. But the movement caused the bells on her cuffs to jingle.

"What in—hold on a minute." Logan squatted down and peered through the tangle of brush. "Who's there?"

Knowing he would spot the bright red of her costume, she scooted back as far as she could, snapping twigs as she went and making her bells jingle again.

"You might as well show yourself," Logan said.

Not waiting for him to drag her out, if that was his intention, she twisted around and dove backward, elbowing her way out the other side, where she tumbled down a pebbled embankment, almost at the feet of a man in an orange jumpsuit, who was working with a rake.

"Hey!" he called.

Not saying anything, except a single "oof" when she landed, she scrambled to her feet. Shuffling along as best she could, she didn't dare to glance back until she'd turned the corner of a utility shed. There she stayed, flattened to the corrugated metal, waiting to catch her breath.

Chapter Eleven

Why had she panicked? Though she'd hoped to keep her job a secret from Logan, under the circumstances she should have made the best of it, identified herself, and explained. They could have laughed about it together.

But then, he and Thea would have laughed too—*at* her, not with her.

Now what? Fortunately her costume wasn't torn, but how did her makeup look? She had no mirror to check, and she couldn't return to her room. But her nose was still in place, thanks to the spirit gum, and her skullcap was still on her head.

After allowing a few minutes, she continued along the garden path and down the flagstone steps as if nothing had happened.

Sunday afternoon had brought out enough children to keep two uniformed child care attendants hopping. There, squatting alongside the fishpond, was a small boy with a headful of orange curls. Patrick.

One of the attendants was trying to convince him to join in the games. "You're frightening the poor fishes, honey," she said. "Don't put your hands in the water."

"I want to hold one."

"Hi there," Ivy said in her Jingles voice. "Let's play swivel-stick with the others."

"No. They're all babies." He plunged a hand in the water again.

Ivy pretended to read his name tag. "It's against the rules to bother the fish, Patrick."

"You don't know anything. Clowns are big stupids." With that he made a scoop of his hands, dipped in, and splashed water in her face. Before she could clear her vision, he raced across the court to where other children were listening to a story about Leo the Lizard, and pushed his way to the front row.

Was it true, Ivy marveled, what Brian, who had originally played Dandy, told her the day he quit? That seeing a giant duck turned some kids into monsters?

Maybe it was the same with clowns. Patrick had been likable and moderately well behaved on their trip yesterday. So why was he out of control now?

As usually happened, one disruptive child affected the others. A water fight broke out, soaking several children, and it was followed by a pummeling match. There was even a bout of tears when a small girl's doll fell in the water.

The three hours Jingles was contracted to spend entertaining, seemed like ten. At last, according to Ivy's trusty watch, time was up. One last game of ringtoss, and she could go to her room and change.

"I win," Patrick cried gleefully, as his ball shot through the wire basket.

"Not fair," came a chorus from the other children. "He stood in front of the rope."

"Try again, Patrick," Ivy coaxed. "Bet you can't do it standing back of the line."

"I already won a prize," he balked.

"You didn't win yet."

"Anybody can stand under the hoop and drop it in." A little boy, whose name tag identified him as Charles, ducked under the rope and demonstrated. "See?"

"C'mon. Try one more time," Ivy begged comically. "Please. For Jingles."

"You're not a clown." He looked up at her, his small chin squared in determination. "You're only a stupid girl. Your name is Ivy."

How had he figured that out? She hadn't done as good a job as she'd thought in disguising her voice.

The others stared at her wide-eyed. "Is your name really Ivy?" Charles asked.

"I'm Jingles," she insisted. "And I can prove it."

"How?" came the chorus.

Ivy did a clown "yuck, yuck, yuck," held up one foot, and shook it to make the bells on her ankles jingle. Then she did a little dance and pretended to fall over her feet. The children laughed.

"Who am I?" she asked, holding a hand to her ear.

"Jingles!" they shouted.

"So who wants to play the game again?" She held a hand to her ear.

"We do!"

"I don't have to play again." Patrick ducked under the ropes, grabbed a plastic bear bank that was to be a prize, and ducked out again. "I already got a prize."

"Make him give it back," the others cried.

"Let him keep it," Ivy said, in the interest of pre-empting a full-fledged tantrum.

When the others yelled their objections, she held up one hand. "The bear Patrick took isn't a winning bear, because he didn't win it."

"It's still a bear," Patrick jeered. "So ha-ha to you."

"Not a special bear. Do you know what makes a winning bear special?"

"What?" the children wanted to know.

"Because if you win—really and truly win—you can take the bear home and put it on a shelf." Ivy went through a pantomime of putting an invisible bear on an invisible shelf. "Every time you look at it, you can say, 'I won you, bear. You're special, so I'm special too.' " She clapped her hands and jumped up and down in glee.

"You can't say that, Patrick," a little girl told him, sticking her tongue in the gap where she'd lost two teeth. " 'Cause you didn't really win."

"My bear looks the same," he argued.

Ivy held up one hand, then with exaggerated movement reached in a box, pulled out a sticker that said NUMBER ONE, and pressed it on a second plastic bear's chest. "There! This bear is Number One. So he's the real, true winner."

"Let me try," said the little girl, and the others lined up behind her.

Patrick shuffled over and sat on a low stone wall, glowering. When the game was over and the children had scattered, he approached again, dragging his feet.

"Your name is *too* Ivy." He crossed his arms over his chest. "My mother told me."

"How does your mother know my name?"

"Because Uncle Logan told her."

Ivy swallowed hard. "And how does Uncle Logan know?"

" 'Cause he got you this job, that's how."

Serious now, Ivy stooped down in front of him, dropping her clown voice. "Logan told you he got me this job?"

"He told Mommy he felt sorry for you. You lost your other job, so you have to be a stupid old clown. If you're mean to me, he'll kick you out like he did before."

Outrage roared in Ivy's ears as the little boy skipped away. Outrage had turned to anger by the time she reached the steps and anger had turned to fury by the time she reached the path.

A drone of voices and laughter drifted from the terrace area, where scattered groups of people were having coffee and conversation. Strains of "Smoke Gets in Your Eyes" played softly in the background.

Ivy saw Thea first. The woman wore a creamy silk blouse and a dirndl skirt that reached her ankles. Logan stood to her left, wearing a dark green shirt under a sport coat in a honeycomb weave. On her right stood a man in a white suit who wore steel-rimmed glasses and had a respectable paunch.

Seething, Ivy made her way over to them.

"Well now, what's this?" The man chuckled. "We have entertainment, have we?"

Thea glanced uneasily at Logan.

"I'm Jingles the Clown," Ivy snarled, turning her full attention to Logan. "And you, Mr. McKenna, are an—an egotistical dictator, who can't be happy unless he's pulling everybody's strings."

"Friend of yours, McKenna?" the man asked, letting out a loud guffaw as Ivy flounced back the way she had come.

"Really!" Thea said.

He wouldn't follow, Ivy assured herself. More important would be for him to smooth things over with the man in the white suit.

She was wrong. As she turned the key in her lock, Logan loomed up behind her, pushed through the door, and slammed it behind him.

"What the devil was that all about?" he asked, grasping her shoulders with both hands. His irises glowed, as if from an inner fire. "You made fools of us both."

She twisted away. "I hope so."

"I ought to drag you back and make you explain."

"Why don't you?"

"Because I'd look even more foolish, with you in that getup."

"Then leave, and let me change."

"I'm not moving until I have a sensible explanation."

"You want an explanation?" She moved to the window and stared out at the lily pond, so smooth and calm, in contrast to the tempest brewing inside her. "When I was a senior in high school, I wanted to be in the Orcheses, a special class of modern dance. Only fifteen girls would be picked out of the whole school, and I practiced for weeks, wanting to be ready for the tryouts."

"And?"

"I was one of the chosen."

"Congratulations. Will we get to the point of this story any time in the near future?"

"I was hysterically happy, until I discovered the truth from one of my classmates, who was only too happy to relay it to me. My father had gone to school a few days before, and told the teacher how much it meant to me to be in the group. It was important to him too, he said, because I'd be moping around the house and making everybody miserable otherwise. It worked, because he and the teacher's husband were fishing buddies. I quit the class.''

''You should have stayed and proved yourself,'' Logan said.

''You don't get it, do you?'' she lashed out. ''I wanted to do it for myself.''

No longer angry, Logan shifted his stance. ''I was trying to help.''

''Like my father was trying to help?'' She crossed her arms and rubbed them as if she were cold. ''It's only one of many such stories if you have a few hours to listen.''

''I understand what you're saying, Ivy. But in this case, I can't see any harm done.''

''The day I visited Thea, she accused me of wanting a handout. I told her she was wrong.''

''This wasn't a handout. Because of me, you lost the income from Toluca Woods. Replacing that income, at least partly, was the right thing to do.''

He made so much sense, the power began to seep out of her anger. ''Why didn't you consult me? Why did you have someone from the convention committee send me a letter?''

''It was their idea, after I did a little explaining.''

''You mean, after you twisted a few arms.''

Silence. He stared at a still life painting over the television—green and gold apples in a wooden bowl. ''Okay. But turning it around, why didn't you tell me that you were on a job here?''

"You already knew."

He pointed a finger at her. "But you didn't know I knew."

What kind of logic was that? "It was your lie first."

"Your lie, mine. What difference does it make?" he muttered, reaching for her, and reaching again, successfully this time. "Haven't we come too far, you and I, to walk away from each other over this?"

He was partly right, she knew the moment she was in the sanctuary of his arms. Her throat constricted, and she hugged him closer still. "I'm sorry I embarrassed you in front of your business associates. I was so—so . . ."

"Forget it." He nudged her head back to collect a kiss, but instead, twisted his face comically. "I'm sorry. I can't bring myself to kiss a clown."

In the heat of their exchange, she'd forgotten she was in makeup. Quickly, she reached up to remove the red ball that was her nose.

"That's a start. How do you get that stuff off?"

"With cold cream. I'll do it when you leave."

"Too late." Catching her wrist, he drew her along with him to the dresser, and he picked up a jar. "This is cold cream?" When she nodded, he unscrewed the lid, plucked a tissue from the box, and set to work with gentle rubbing, giving special attention to her mouth.

"Give it to me." She tried to take the tissue, but he held it out of reach until she gave up, then went to work again.

''That'll do it,'' he said finally.

''Satisfied?''

''If I'm forgiven.'' His breath ruffled her hair.

''For what?'' she asked, no longer able to remember why she'd been so miffed at him.

The brushing of their mouths was feathery light at first, then moved to eager acceptance, and shared joy.

''How are you going to explain the scene in the garden to Thea?'' she asked finally.

''Nothing you do would surprise Thea.'' Logan smiled down at her.

Did that mean Ivy had often been a topic of their discussions? Of course she had been. He'd told Thea details of her job here. They were friends, as well as partners.

But you, silly girl, are here, in his arms.

''Will you be at the party tonight?'' she asked, forcing thoughts of the other woman back.

''I hadn't planned on it.''

''Please.'' Though she hadn't thought of needing company when she'd attended the other meetings, tonight was different. She was different, and so was Logan.

''I'll try.''

''Don't try,'' she said. ''Be there. At least for one dance.''

''That's an order?'' He exhaled deeply. ''I'd better get going then, if I'm going to get business tied up. Why don't you lie down and take a nap? You need your beauty sleep with a face like that.''

"My face." In the heat of their argument, and their making up afterward, she'd forgotten how she must look. Logan had wiped away most of the clown makeup, but there would be streaky remnants. "I must look terrible."

"Terrible," he agreed.

"How could you stand to look at me?" she asked.

He frowned. "I kept my eyes closed most of the time."

"You didn't!"

"No," he said, serious again. "I didn't."

Chapter Twelve

" "We thought you'd disappeared off the face of the earth." The woman from the pet shop was wearing a floor-length dress of chartreuse crinkle crepe.

Her husband wore a string tie and cowboy boots. "You missed some good meetings."

"I know. I've been busy."

The woman jabbed her husband in the ribs with her elbow. "That hunk with the killer smile? I don't blame you for missing a few speeches."

Difficult as it was for Ivy to muster enthusiasm, as she watched for Logan, knowing from experience that he might not appear, she accepted dances with everyone who asked, earning a few bruised toes in the process. Time passed, and the hands of the clock moved nearer and nearer the hour that marked the end of the celebration.

"I hope you appreciate the fact that I detest and abominate these affairs," Logan said, appearing at her elbow as she'd begun to give up hope.

"I do," she said, marveling at how the sight of him could light up a room for her.

"Ready for that dance I promised?" he asked, leading her onto the floor.

"Why do you detest and abominate last-night celebrations?" she wanted to know.

"Because everyone is saying good-bye to everyone, and little business is accomplished."

"And business is all that matters?"

"Business is why we're here."

"You don't like to dance?" He hadn't seemed to mind dancing with Thea.

"Not inside a fishbowl. There are people here who'll consider it a slight if I don't ask them to dance too." With effort, he returned the smile of a woman in a gray satin pantsuit, and mouthed a cheery "Hello, nice to see you too."

"Why shouldn't you dance if it means so much to them?"

He held her at arm's length. "Are you trying to get rid of me?"

"What do you think?"

"I think you're trying to pick another fight," he teased.

"Why would I do that?"

"Because you want a replay of the way we made up last time."

Memories of their last kiss flickered through her mind. She could feel the heat creeping up to her neck, and knew she was blushing. "Did you have trouble finding me in the crowd?"

"None," he said, guiding her gracefully from one step to another, to the strains of a song she'd always loved, but whose name she couldn't remember now. "You stand out, whether you're wearing a clown costume or a pair of blue jeans. But in that dress, you can take a man's breath away."

The dress was ice-blue shantung, with a shorter skirt than she was accustomed to wearing. She'd bought it the week before the convention, and had paid more than she should have. With Logan's pronounced approval, she no longer bewailed the payments she'd be making for the next few months.

As they made a series of turns, she caught sight of Thea, beautiful too in a white crepe dress that bared one shoulder, and pearl earrings. She'd only just arrived too. Did that mean she and Logan had been together?

And if they had? Ivy pressed her face into his shoulder.

He didn't say anything more until the song was over. Yet, from his distracted manner, in spite of his comments on her dress, she knew he wasn't overcome by the romantic music. Was it only that she'd forced him to be here tonight? She didn't think so.

"Is something wrong?" she asked.

Not answering at first, he led her through two more

turns in the line of direction away from the crowd, then off the floor. "I spoke with Clarice Nicholson. She said you agreed to supply a dancing dog for the opening of her store in the new Willow Lake Center."

"Isn't it wonderful? Meeting her opened a whole new path for me."

"You weren't aware that Willow Lake is a Mc-Kenna & Howard property?"

Her body began to tense even before her mind grasped the meaning behind his words. "I didn't think about it."

"The stores in this particular mall are elegant, you might say, catering to a more selective customer," he went on, a stiffness in his voice that she hadn't noticed earlier. "There aren't any—"

"Pizza parlors," she interrupted, as he searched for the word he wanted.

"That's right. Nothing that caters to children."

"I'll put a rhinestone collar on Toodles." She kept her eyes away from his. "Have you told Clarice how you feel?"

"It might work to better advantage, if you called and backed out of your arrangement."

The orchestra had began to play "I'll See You in My Dreams."

"Why is that?"

"It's a sticky situation." He walked her still farther from the dance floor. "Nicholson Industries is into a dozen other businesses that deal with us. Not just candy. There are gift shops, and stationery stores.

Shops that deal with unique kitchenware, as well as linens.''

"In other words, Clarice Nicholson is too important for you to push around." Ivy pulled her arm out of his grasp.

He gaped at her. "Let's not have another scene."

"By all means, let's not." She flashed him a smile that displayed all her teeth, as she backed away.

"As usual, you're taking this wrong," he muttered.

"I'm taking it exactly as you meant it," she said. "And you can take this exactly as I mean it. Do your worst, Mr. McKenna. But unless Clarice Nicholson tells me otherwise, Toodles the Poodle will be fulfilling his contract at Willow Lake as scheduled."

The woman in the gray satin pantsuit had noticed Logan, and was heading toward them.

Logan looked toward her, and back at Ivy. "As you can see, I have to dance, as long as I'm here."

"Poor baby."

"We'll bat this around in the morning, on the way back to St. Louis."

"That's what you think," Ivy murmured, hurrying to her room alone.

Was she doing something she'd regret? she thought only briefly, as she snapped her packed suitcases shut. Would the planned trip together have given her and Logan a chance to work out this disagreement? Not a chance.

A few kisses, a hug or two, and he'd actually expected her to react as if she were a robot. He'd flicked the switch to set her in motion. How could she have convinced herself that he'd changed?

After returning her room key to the front desk, she got in her car and started the long drive home.

"Is that the last customer?" Ivy called, when she heard the Party Animal door close.

"Yes, thank goodness. I'll never get supper on the table tonight." Florence flipped the sign in the window to CLOSED and went back to the counter to get her handbag and books. "It was better when we didn't have so many customers. I don't have time to study on the job anymore."

"You won't hear me complaining." Ivy pulled the chain that turned off the light to the storage room. "If those jobs for Nicholson Industries don't fall through, and if business continues, it'll be smooth sailing."

"Listen to you. If, if, if. Why should they fall through? Mrs. Nicholson wants Toodles, not only for the opening, but for all the holiday weekends through the year."

"I know." Ivy hadn't told Florence about Logan's attempt to sabotage the jobs, and the attempts he could still be making to stop her. "Guess I tend to look on the negative side."

"Did you notice though," Florence said, turning the pages of the desk calendar, "that the date of the Nicholson opening coincides with the date of the fair in Sedalia?"

"It's okay."

"How can it be okay? Scott can't be in two places at once. The kid you've been using for Toodles moved out of state, that magician guy won't stoop to wearing a poodle outfit, and the new girl went with her family on vacation."

"I'll work the Sedalia date myself."

Florence clutched the edge of the counter in exaggerated dismay. "Tell me you're joking."

"I promised to drive to Sedalia for Dad's birthday anyway. Why should I lay out extra money for gas and a hotel for someone else, when I can handle it? I don't mind another couple of days in a duck suit."

"You came back from that convention looking as if you'd been run over by a truck. It was days before I could get a sensible answer out of you."

"It wasn't the clown suit that did me in."

"What then?"

Though more than two weeks had passed since the convention, Ivy still couldn't bear to think about what had happened between her and Logan, let alone talk about it.

"Meeting all those people was grueling."

"You like meeting people," Florence argued. "Oh, that reminds me, Mrs. Nicholson wants Toodles to do the Highland fling periodically, in front of the store. You know, in keeping with the Scottish theme of their logo?"

"Scott's inventive. I'm sure he can do a dance that'll pass."

"I've seen it done. It's something like this." Florence put one hand on her hip, the other in the air, and began touching the toe of one foot on the floor in front, then in back, as she hopped in place.

"You aren't perchance auditioning, are you?"

"Bite your tongue. Mrs. Candy Store also wants Toodles to wear a plaid cap. She sent one in the Nicholson tartan by messenger."

"I didn't see it."

"You weren't here when it arrived." Florence shrugged. "I stuck it in the wardrobe with the rest of the costumes. What with hitting myself over the head with those math equations, I forgot. Did you have a chance to check my homework yet?"

"You got all but two right."

"Yes!" Florence shook both fists in the air.

As Ivy headed back to the stock room, she smiled at the older woman's determination to succeed. "I'd better make sure that cap is big enough for Toodles's head. Did you call Scott to verify the date?"

"Oops." Florence grimaced. "I'll do it now."

"Please. He could make other plans, and we'd be up a creek."

"Right on."

"Be sure to stress how important this particular job is, and how it can mean the difference between success and failure."

"Will do. I'll tell him about the dance."

"And the hat."

Florence put on her reading glasses, and began to flip the phone cards in the file box.

As Ivy had suspected, the plaid tam was a mite small, and would have to be basted in place if it was going to stay on Toodles's shaggy head. Maybe she should take it home and do it tonight.

All the activity lately had kept both her and Florence hopping. Since the ads she'd placed in the *Bargain Mailer*, and the additional notice the shop had received when Scott went forth wearing a sandwich board proclaiming the fun of shopping at Party Animal, business had tripled.

She'd also adapted an idea from one of the convention speeches, and persuaded the man at the mailbox store next door to allow a Party Animal ad on the south side of his building, where it could be seen from the main street.

"It'll help us both," she said. "They'll stop to buy party paraphernalia, and notice your mailing service."

Poor Scott, she thought, rummaging through her closet shelf for the sewing kit. Though he liked getting the money, she'd been working him relentlessly. She'd conducted a few interviews for more helpers, but hadn't yet found anybody she felt good about sending on the job.

The phone rang and, wondering who would be calling this late, she went to the door and listened.

"Party Animal. May I help you? Yes, she is. Just a minute." Florence held a hand over the mouthpiece. "Logan McKenna wants to talk to you."

"No," Ivy mouthed, waving her hands.

"I already said you were here."

"Tell him you were mistaken."

"Sorry. We're closed," Florence said in her proper telephone operator voice. "Ms. Canfield just stepped out the door. No, she already drove away. I'm sorry."

"Did he say what he wanted?" It was a bit late in the game for Logan to try to cancel Toodles's performance. But then, he couldn't have achieved such success in his field if he hadn't been relentless.

"No, and he didn't sound pleased. Isn't he Mc-Kenna of McKenna and Howard?"

"The same."

Florence twisted her mouth to one side. "Hmmm."

"Don't say it," Ivy warned her, returning to her search again.

"Ivy!" It sounded more like a bark than a summons, but Ivy recognized it even before Logan came to meet her from the stairs where he'd been waiting. "I could get the President on the telephone easier than I can get you."

"What did I do now?" She kept walking.

"I want to know why you left me stranded at the hotel. Do you have any idea how much trouble you caused?"

"No, but I suppose you're going to tell me." She set the plastic bag that held Toodles's head on the landing, and opened the screen door.

"I'd already made arrangements for someone to drive my car back. They'd gone by the time I realized you'd checked out."

She made a clicking sound with her tongue. "And you had to hitchhike home?"

His eyes blazed. "You're lucky I didn't."

"You must have found wheels, or you wouldn't be here. May I go inside now?"

He grabbed the edge of the door. "By all means. Let's."

"I don't remember inviting you."

"We have to talk."

"You're always saying that, aren't you? When we talk, I get the worst of it."

"Because you won't face the facts. For one, I'm the bad guy because I think your animal characters don't belong in a shopping mall. At the same time, you won't admit that you're embarrassed about dressing up as one."

"Not true."

"Then why did you hide in the bushes when you saw me coming at the hotel? You hoped I wouldn't catch you in costume." His laugh was harsh.

"You knew I was there?"

"How could I not know? One minute I saw polka dots, and suddenly they were gone. Then there were bells jingling in the bushes, and you tumbled out on the other side."

"Why didn't you mention it before?"

"You didn't want me to know, so I played along. Tell me, Ms. Canfield, is your father aware of your performances? Or do you keep it secret from him too?"

That was a low blow. "He knows about Toodles."

"But does he know that you, the proprietor of Party Animal, make a habit of dressing like a duck?"

"I love to do make-believe with children and see them laugh. Don't judge everyone by yourself." She folded her arms and looked up at him. "Were you ever a little boy, Logan?"

"You're child enough for both of us."

"You're wrong there too, I'm not one of your little sisters."

"Have I behaved as if you were?"

"You don't have to comb my hair and send me off to school. You don't have to tell me how to run my shop—as if you have the answer to everything. Actually, you haven't got a clue. What experience have you had in retail?"

"Basic rules apply to any business."

"So say you."

He turned away, and turned back again. "It's the oddest thing, Ivy. But even when you're behaving like a spoiled brat, I have this—this uncontrollable desire to kiss you."

"Take a couple of aspirin, and call me in the morning."

Snarling, he caught her in his arms. "That's enough."

With a cry of dismissal, she tried to extricate herself, but she thudded against his chest anyway. In an attempt to avoid his lips, she turned her head from one side to the other, back again, and again. But before long, her efforts weakened.

Her protests dwindled. His lips found hers, and she was lost. Even as she returned his kiss, anger pulsed through her.

"This can't happen," she said breathlessly.

"You're right," he whispered. "Not here."

"Not anywhere. Go home." She slid her hands between them again, and pushed with all her strength.

His laugh was dry. "You kiss me the way you did a minute ago, and tell me to go home?"

"I won't let you in." she cried. "You've manipulated me for the last time."

The door across the hall creaked open, and the same elderly tenant looked out. "Is everything all right, Ivy?"

"Yes," Ivy said tightly. "Mr. McKenna was just leaving."

"Humph." The woman eased the door closed again, but a shuffling sound said she was standing on the other side of it, listening.

"I've been hanging around here so long waiting, she wrote down my license plate number earlier."

"She didn't!" Ivy managed a quivery smile.

"You think it's funny?" He drew his lips into a straight, thin line. "Maybe it is. You accuse me of manipulation, when you're the expert."

"I manipulated *you*?"

"That night at the river, the way you looked, all

soft and helpless. Later, the way you kissed me. Not to mention your behavior at the convention, when . . .''

"Stop it."

"You expected me to cave in, and give you what you wanted."

"What did I want?" she asked, stung.

"Toluca Woods." His words dripped with contempt. "And a few other choice locations for Dandy."

"That isn't true—exactly." To deny his accusation would have been a lie. While she'd wanted to be with him, she'd hoped at the same time that he'd have a change of heart. "It wasn't like that."

"Wasn't it?" He jerked his head toward the other apartment. "I'd better leave before your Neighborhood Watch calls the police."

Chapter Thirteen

The fairgrounds were crowded on Thursday and Friday. The children who came up to receive a balloon were so appreciative, Ivy was inspired to perform all the acrobatics in her limited range. A few preteens tried to unnerve her, but they weren't vicious. They were only showing off for their peers.

She wouldn't have minded if her job in Sedalia lasted twice as long, except for her father's suspicions about where she went every day.

On the pretense of visiting friends, she left after breakfast, put her costume on in the van, and took it off again before she returned.

"Out again?" Her father looked at her over the top of his newspaper. "I thought you came to spend some time with us."

"We celebrated your birthday on Wednesday," she

reminded him. "And I was here to help get the food on the table."

"It isn't the food, darn it. You didn't see your friends this much when you lived at home."

"Your father's right, honey," Sylvia Canfield agreed. "We never get to see you."

"I was here long enough to beat you at a game of chess," Ivy reminded him. She got up and put her arms around his neck.

"Big deal," he said, hunching her away.

Surreptitiously she glanced at her watch. "I have to call the shop. But I'll put the charges on my card."

"You don't even get away from that place when you're away from it," he grumbled.

"Isn't that how it is with you and the office?"

"A man's work is his work. It isn't the same."

"It's exactly the same," she chirped.

The phone was busy for at least fifteen minutes, and when Florence finally answered, she was out of breath. "Oh, Ivy, I'm glad you called. We have a genuine problem."

"What?" she asked, before fear got too tight a grip. These days, with Florence a genuine problem could mean she'd flunked a math quiz.

"The candy store opening. I don't have anybody to play Toodles."

"What about Scott?"

"I—I forgot to tell him about it."

"You didn't!"

"I know. Rage at me. You can't make me feel

worse than I do already. But the day you asked me to call, I got distracted and it slipped my mind. Or what's left of my mind these days.''

''Forget all that.'' Ivy tried to sound more calm than she felt. ''Call Scott now.''

''Don't you think I have? All last night when I realized what I'd done, and all this morning. There's no answer.''

Ivy squeezed her eyes shut. ''Could you possibly play Toodles? I realize I'm asking a lot. But at this point, it's just the idea of somebody showing up in a poodle suit and giving out balloons.''

''Heck, I considered it. But my car is in the shop and I don't have transportation way out there.''

''Couldn't your husband drive you?''

''He's gone to a baseball game. I called the bus company, but it would mean transferring three times, and me dressed up in a dog suit?''

There had to be an answer. ''Dig out the applications. Call the kids who applied for a job.''

''All I get are rings or busy signals.''

''How about Brian?''

''He hung up on me.''

Ivy looked at the clock and groaned. ''Toodles is supposed to be at the mall in an hour and fifteen minutes.''

''I know, I know. I'll keep trying Scott. Maybe he'll come home. Keep your fingers crossed.''

''And my toes.'' Ivy rubbed a place between her eyebrows as if she could erase this new trouble. ''Even if I left here now, I wouldn't get back in time to do any good.''

"I'm sorry."

"Don't be sorry. Keep trying. I'll call you from the fairgrounds, the first chance I get. If you haven't found a substitute by then, you'd better call Mrs. Nicholson and explain."

"What'll I tell her?"

"I don't know. If we let her down on this first assignment, she'll never trust us again, and the other jobs are as good as lost."

"What if I tell her everybody's sick? She'd have to accept it as an act of God, wouldn't she?"

"An act of God is a tornado or an earthquake."

"Maybe we'll be lucky and have one."

"Florence!"

"What's up?" Mr. Canfield asked, having heard part of the conversation.

"My poodle can't make the opening of a candy store."

"What do you expect?" He snorted. "People willing to make fools of themselves for minimum wage can't be counted on as far as you can throw them."

"*I've* worked for minimum wage."

"My point exactly."

"Arthur!" Sylvia sounded shocked. "Your father didn't mean that."

"I know." Ivy tried to sound cheery. "I'll see you two later.

"Don't forget we eat supper at seven," Sylvia

called. "We're having tuna casserole, and it doesn't wait."

The sun was warm, but not too warm, and there was even a breeze. The fairgrounds were more crowded today than they had been the previous two days, but Ivy wasn't able manage more than a weak smile for the young man who let her in the employees' gate.

"Dandy rarin' to go?" he asked.

"He's about to kick the side out of the van if I don't let him out."

"Park on the other side of the cookhouse." He pointed. "Then you get over to the grandstand. You're supposed to follow the drum majorettes in the parade."

"Yikes. I forgot the parade."

"Better shake a leg. I can hear the band starting up."

The parade would leave the grounds and weave a path up one street and down another, with participants doing whatever they could think of to make people who crowded the sidewalks follow them back to the ticket booth.

With the many floats, high school bands, costumed horseback riders, and performers, it was almost two hours before Ivy could reach a phone.

The answering machine was on when she dialed the shop, and a taped Florence came on as usual, then added an aside.

"Good news. All is well. Dandy was at Willow Lake with time to spare. Have a good day!"

The release of tension made Ivy laugh until she was weak. Then noticing a boy of about four watching, clearly puzzled by a duck using the telephone, she quacked, and to his delight, turned a somersault, got up, and did a hitch kick.

Yes! Florence had come through for her.

It would never happen again, she promised herself when it was all over, and she was driving back to her parents' house.

Logan had been right about the need to have enough people on call to prevent the panic she and Florence had experienced today. But he'd been wrong when he accused Ivy of being embarrassed about what she did.

She enjoyed dressing up, and probably would occasionally even if she had a full staff. It was fun to put joy on the little ones' faces. His assumption that it was beneath her dignity only pointed out how wrong they were for each other.

Now she had to pull into a gas station, and fill up for her trip home. At the same time, she'd go in the rest room and change her clothes. It had been too crowded at the fairgrounds, and it wasn't easy managing it in the cramped van.

As always, her face was a streaky mess under Dandy's head, and she had to make herself presentable as quickly as possible. Dinner at seven, her mother had said.

A splash of cool water felt good on her face. She removed the pins that held her hair in place and shook her head to free it.

Hold on a minute, she told her reflection. *If Logan is so wrong, why are you taking such pains to hide what you're doing from your parents?*

Panic flickered through her briefly, as Ivy turned into the Canfield driveway, headed toward the kitchen, and smelled her mother's tuna casserole. For the space of a dozen heartbeats, she was twelve years old, and late for Saturday supper again. Her father was ready with a stern lecture about being on time, and how when he was a boy, a latecomer to the table went to bed without his supper.

Reminding herself of the decision she'd made as she drove home, she got out, still wearing her costume, except for the head, which she carried.

Arthur Canfield was watching a game show on television when she came in, and Sylvia was setting plates on the table.

"Supper smells good," Ivy said brightly. Actually, it did, though her mother's casserole, invariably with soggy potato chips as topping, had never been her favorite fare.

Her father glanced up to acknowledge her entrance, then gripped the edge of his chair.

"She's trying the costume on to see how it works. You know, for her shop?" Sylvia said uneasily. "It's very cute."

"I already know how it works, Mother," Ivy said breezily. "I've worn it eight hours a day for the last three days at the fair. That's why I'd like a shower if you can hold dinner a bit longer."

"You walked around at the fair dressed in a duck costume?" her mother asked. "I thought you hired schoolboys for that."

"And schoolgirls. I usually do. But since I was here for Daddy's birthday anyway, I thought I'd save money. Besides, I like doing it. When Dandy makes a child laugh, I feel good inside. That's a bonus that comes with the job."

"You told us you were visiting friends," Sylvia accused.

"I thought the truth might upset you."

"You got that right." Her father snorted. "How could you pull a stunt like this in your hometown? I run a business. What if somebody saw you?"

"They didn't recognize me—until I introduced myself as Art Canfield's daughter," she teased.

"Wha-aat?" His eyes bulged beneath his glasses.

"Just joking. I wouldn't, if you didn't want me to." Ivy went on to explain how well the shop was doing, and how the fund for the balloon payment was growing. "If I had confessed earlier, you could have come to the fairgrounds and watched me in action."

"I'd dance on the lawn in my BVDs first," he growled. "Would you mind taking that—that thing off? I can't carry on a sensible conversation with Donald Duck."

"I'm not Donald. I'm Dandy."

"Donald, Dandy, it's all the same."

She dug in her handbag, pulled out a pocket-sized notebook, and handed it to him with a flourish.

"That's my projected income for the next few months. If you'll notice, I'm almost there."

He studied the book for a long moment, turned the page, and turned it back again. "You can make this much dressing like a duck?"

"Some of it comes from Dandy and Toodles and their buddies. But sales have been improving at the shop too."

"That's wonderful, honey," Sylvia said. "Would you change clothes now, please? The casserole will get cold."

"Right away." She kissed the bald spot on top of her father's head. "Give me five minutes."

"My daughter, the duck," he grumbled, not sounding nearly so upset as she'd expected him to be.

"Quack-quack, Daddy," she said, then hurried upstairs to shower and dress.

Released from his carrier, Spiffy strolled from one end of the shop to the other, crouching under counters, leaping in the display window and onto the chairs, wanting to make sure nothing had gone amiss during his absence. Satisfied, he nosed open the bathroom door and jumped in the shower stall for a snooze.

Ivy turned the radio on and settled down to work, Florence had classes that day and wouldn't be coming in, but she'd left another apology on the message spindle.

To make up for my stupidity, she'd scrawled, *I agree to wear a sandwich board one day next week—free of charge. If you promise not to tell my husband and children.*

Ivy giggled to herself and shuffled through the rest of the messages. Someone had called from the blue-grass festival wanting price quotes. A woman Ivy had spoken with the day before she left for Sedalia wanted to discuss her husband's birthday festivities. Could Ivy work along with her caterer?

Neither call required an immediate answer, and she decided to wait until the shop was empty before tying herself up on the phone.

While she waited, she'd sweep up a spill of confetti at the end of aisle two before it was tracked all over the store. Someone had broken open the bag, dropped it, then too embarrassed to confess, had fled, leaving the mess behind.

"I'll be in the back," she told the handful of brows-ers who remained. A party shop, she'd learned, was like a bookstore. People often came just to look. But if treated cordially, they returned to make purchases. "When you're ready, ring the bell."

As long as she had the broom, she'd sweep the storeroom. Someone had left cabinet drawers open, and hangers lay on the floor. Here and there were curls from Toodles's costume. Scott was usually better or-ganized. But by the time Florence was able to contact him, he would have been in a hurry to get dressed.

The empty space in the closet said that he hadn't returned his costume yet, and he'd neglected to take the check she'd made out to him and left in a marked envelope. That wasn't like him either.

When she'd dealt with the last customer, she dialed his house and got his mother.

"Hi, Ivy," the woman said. "Scott and some other kids went to Branson for the weekend and decided to stay over."

"He couldn't have. He worked Willow Center Saturday."

"Not Scotty. He left Friday afternoon, about two."

"You're sure?"

"As sure as I am that they cleaned out the refrigerator making sandwiches to take with them."

"Then who . . ." As she thought about it, she remembered that Florence hadn't said who she hired, only that Toodles was at work and all was well. "Never mind. Thanks."

A truck with the shipment of paper plates and tablecloths she'd been expecting arrived as she was about to eat lunch. As she was struggling with scissors that needed sharpening, and yards of impossibly tough tape that sealed the boxes, a car screeched into the curb. Logan's car.

"No." She pressed a fist to her mouth. She wasn't ready yet to face him.

Chapter Fourteen

Did Logan plan to list Toodles's sins one by one, and issue an ultimatum that the dog wouldn't be allowed to darken his mall again? If so, she'd inform him, as she had at their last two meetings, to take it up with Clarice Nicholson.

"What are you doing here?" he asked, looking as surprised to see her as she was to see him. "I thought you were in Sedalia."

"I'm back."

"Where's Florence?" He looked past her.

Ivy put down the scissors. "Since when do you know Florence?"

"I know her," he said ruefully. "Believe me, I know her."

What did that mean? "How may I help you?" she asked in her deliberately cordial shopkeeper's voice.

He approached the counter, and picked up one of the trick pens he'd played with before. ''I only wanted to tell you that you'd won.''

''That's nice to hear. But what have I won?''

''The candy store is on the second level of the shopping plaza at Willow Lake. There wasn't a problem with kids running in front of cars, or stopping traffic the way they did at Toluca Woods. The escalators are located on the sides of the building, and I don't foresee any problems in the future.''

''You were at the shopping center Saturday?''

''My job is to make sure things run smoothly.''

She was painfully aware of that. ''You could have called and told me.''

His skin was more tan than it had been when she saw him last, as if he'd spent time in the sun. With Thea? It had a faint sheen from the heat of the day, and under his sport coat, he was wearing the forest green shirt she liked.

Earth tones suited him. Greens in all shades, tans and browns. Ivory and cream. Any color at all, actually.

The silence that fell between them was anything but silent. The air crackled and pulsed as they considered each other. She had kissed, and been kissed by, that wonderful mouth. She'd been cradled in those beautifully muscled arms.

''I wanted to tell you in person.'' He stood for a moment, his expression troubled, as if he wanted to say more. Then he gave up, and started away.

"Leave the pen," she called after him.

He patted his pocket, and laid the pen on the counter. "Sorry about that."

"I imagine you collect a lot of pens that way."

He touched two fingers to his forehead in a kind of cowboy salute. The gesture looked so final, she wanted to forget her reservations, grab him, and hold on. But she wouldn't.

Instead, she trailed him to the door. "If you thought I was in Sedalia, how did you plan to tell me in person?"

"I expected to tell Florence. As long is she isn't hiding out from me too, she could have relayed the message."

"That's another thing. How do you know Florence?"

"Why all the questions?"

"You ask plenty of your own."

"I suppose I do." He grasped the doorknob, but didn't turn it. "Good luck with everything, Ivy."

A pickup truck with a blaring radio made a U-turn and parked behind Logan's car. A man in cutoff shorts got out. Leaving his motor running, he strode into the mailbox store next door, singing tunelessly and slapping a hand against his leg in time with the music.

The truck, which came around every afternoon at the same time, had been in so many accidents it was impossible to make out its original lines. The paint job, a flat fuchsia with monster faces painted on the door, contrasted sharply with Logan's immaculately kept metallic green car, the midday sun glinting off the polished chrome.

Something in the backseat caught Ivy's gaze, and not understanding, she edged closer to the window. Round blue eyes and curly white hair? "Is somebody else in the car?"

Logan shook his head.

"Yes, there is," she insisted. "And it's somebody I know."

"Ivy . . ."

"Who's in the car, Logan?" She slid in front of him to bar his way.

Sighing, he pulled back. "Okay. You found me out. I expected Florence to be here when I came to return the costume. She promised no one would know. Especially you."

"Return the costume?" She held out one hand. "Let me understand this. *You* played Toodles at Willow Lake Center?"

He pivoted on his heel, and faced the rear of the shop. "I'll take a cup of coffee, if you have it."

"Not until you explain."

"I had the misfortune of coming here Saturday morning. When I introduced myself, your clerk turned into a madwoman."

"She did what?"

"She needed my help, she said. Naturally I agreed— before she told me what she had in mind."

"When she told you, you didn't back out?"

"I got as far as the door, but she started to cry."

He grimaced. "She said she'd lose her job. She was trying to put herself through college. It wasn't easy to find employment these days—especially for a woman her age."

"That worked?" Amazing.

"I could only think how hard it was for my mother when Dad left, and she had to go back to school so she could get a decent job."

"Florence was crying?" Ivy couldn't imagine it, unless the woman had been imitating the heroine of her favorite soap opera.

"Buckets. There wasn't time to get anyone else, she said. It was my fault because I'd cut off so much of your income. If Toodles didn't show up in time, you'd lose the candy store. If you lost the candy store, you'd lose the shop."

"And you gave in?"

"What else could I do? No one would recognize me in a dog suit, as long as I kept my mouth shut. And it would only be for a few hours."

"You played Toodles," she repeated numbly, still unable to believe what she was hearing.

"McToodles," he corrected. "It wasn't until I had the costume on that she broke the news about the Highland fling."

Ivy pressed her hands to her mouth to keep from laughing. It didn't work.

"Don't say anything. Not a word. Now may I have that coffee?"

Overwhelmed with tenderness, she nodded, and led

the way to the back of the shop. ''You claim Florence jumped on you when you came to the shop. Why did you come here in the first place?'' After their last encounter she was certain she'd never see him again.

''Patrick asked me to return a plastic bank he took from you at the convention. A bear. He was upset, because you said he hadn't really won it.''

Good for Patrick. Experience had shown her that children were basically fair, unless taught to be otherwise. ''You came just for that?''

''And to leap down your throat for being so hard on a fatherless six-year-old.''

After the sacrifice Logan had made for her, he deserved to sound off a bit. She folded her arms, and waited. ''Go ahead and leap.''

''I changed my mind.'' He slapped a hand to his forehead and exhaled. ''I got a glimpse of Patrick the Terrible.''

''Uh-oh.''

''He showed up at the plaza, and when Thea wasn't looking, kept sticking pins in my balloons, popping them right and left.''

''What did you do?''

''What could I do, without giving myself away— except make the best of it?''

''Exactly.''

''But when he started pulling my tail, and got the other kids doing it, I couldn't take any more.'' Logan held up one hand, palm toward her. ''I took him aside, and explained in no uncertain terms about the treatment of animals, giant or otherwise. Thea was about as furious as I've ever seen her.''

"Because you scolded Patrick?"

"Because I was wearing a dog suit."

"She thought a client might recognize you and it would make your company look bad?"

"No. She was convinced I only did it because I'm in love with you."

Ivy blinked. "But you set her straight?"

"She already had it straight." Logan's eyes met hers straight on, and speckles of gray swirled through the intense green of his irises.

"You explained, didn't you," Ivy asked, "that Florence reminded you of your mother?"

He laughed under his breath. "She knows it would take a heck of a lot more incentive than that."

Meaning—what? Heat that had been building in her chest since his arrival, was crawling up her neck to her face. At the same time, her backbone felt as if it were made of ice. "Was Patrick upset?"

"Not after we straightened things out. In fact, he thought it was 'awesome' that his uncle was McToodles the Poodle, and his aunt was Dandy Duck."

"His aunt?" she questioned.

"When he saw us kissing on the boat, he assumed we were getting married, remember?"

"But you explained."

"What was there to explain? We *will* get married eventually, you and I. It's inevitable." His tone was matter-of-fact.

Her mouth sagged. "You haven't even asked me."

"No need to. The answer is in the depths of those sea-blue eyes."

"Aren't you taking a lot for granted?"

"I walked through fire for you, Ivy. I even did a dance that made members of the original Nicholson clan turn over in their graves. What more could you want?"

"I don't know. Unless . . ."

"Unless what?"

"Since you don't do much at the malls except stand over others, and make sure they're working . . ."

"I don't do much?"

"I keep a list of people who can be here for rush calls. If I have a cancellation, and need a replacement clown or poodle. Would you like to be on it?"

"I'll forget you asked that," he said, leaning down to kiss her soundly.

"Admit it, Logan," she said, taking a moment to recover her speech. "You enjoyed it, didn't you?"

"Immensely," he said, leaning toward her again.

"I don't mean the kiss. I mean the playacting. Dressing in costume, playing with children, and knowing they're having fun because of you."

"I'd rather know they're having fun because of another poor misguided sap, in another dog costume."

"You don't mean that."

"I've never meant anything more. Unless . . ."

"Another unless?"

"Unless it's the fact that I'm thoroughly and completely in love with you, Ivy Canfield, and have been from the moment I saw you.''

''Beak, tail feathers, and all?'' she questioned, biting back a cry of supreme happiness.

A smile twitched at the corners of his mouth. ''Let me revise that statement. I've been in love with you from the moment I saw you—as you are.''

''What about our arguments?''

''We never argue,'' he said quickly.

''If that's the case, I suppose Dandy's free to return to work at Toluca Woods.''

''You suppose wrong,'' he said sternly, his eyes darkening. ''We have to draw the line somewhere. Business is business and this is . . .''

''Yes?''

His gaze caressed her face and settled on her mouth. ''This is something entirely different.''

She met his kiss halfway, sliding her hands up his arms and lacing them behind his neck.

Clearly she had a thing or two to learn about Logan McKenna. But he had a thing or two to learn about himself too. A week ago, who could have convinced him that he'd be wearing a dog suit, and dancing the Highland fling at a shopping mall?

So she wouldn't argue about it now. There was plenty of time, and Dandy was in no hurry.